SLIMED

SLIMED

LIAM GRAY

SCHOLASTIC INC.

All rights reserved. Published by Scholastic Inc., *Publishers since 1920*. SCHOLASTIC and associated logos are trademarks and/or registered trademarks of Scholastic Inc.

The publisher does not have any control over and does not assume any responsibility for author or third-party websites or their content.

This book is a work of fiction. Names, characters, places, and incidents are either the product of the author's imagination or are used fictitiously, and any resemblance to actual persons, living or dead, business establishments, events, or locales is entirely coincidental.

ISBN 978-1-338-62072-6

10 9 8 7 6 5 4 3 2 1   21 22 23 24 25

Printed in the U.S.A.   40
First printing 2021

Book design by Baily Crawford

For those seeking top-secret answers

(Warning: Don't let your parents
eat your homework)

CHAPTER ONE

(Billy)

On the third day of fourth grade, the teacher went around and made everyone in our class say what their favorite part of school was. I've always hated being singled out like that, so when it got to me I sort of panicked and—bad idea—told him the truth. I told him my favorite part of school was when it was over.

That got a note sent home to my parents. The first of *many*.

But hey, was I wrong? The end of the day is the best. All the rules get flipped, and suddenly it's okay to talk, and run around, and stop paying attention, and—if you live close, like me—walk right off school property.

That was my *really* favorite part: the moment I crossed that invisible line. Because school couldn't follow me home.

Well, not normally it couldn't. It did last Wednesday, though.

"Hey! Billy! Billy Hamilton! Wait up!"

I'd only just made it across the street when I looked back.

Sam Baptiste was racing down the school steps toward me, her backpack bouncing along with the colorful beads in her braids.

I groaned, but I stopped and waited for her. There was no point trying to escape. Not only was Sam a really fast runner, but her mom was our school principal. If I took off, her mom would definitely hear about it, and I'd already seen the principal too many times that year. In fact, the last time she'd told me that if my grades didn't improve, I wasn't going to pass fourth grade.

One parent-teacher conference later I'd been signed up for every extra-credit assignment that came along. A week after that, I was Sam's science partner for the most annoying project imaginable.

"I can't believe you forgot we were meeting after class!" Sam yelled, waiting for the crossing guard to let her across the street. "We've only got three days left before tryouts!"

When the guard finally raised her flag, Sam raced across, pulling a piece of paper from her pocket and shoving it right

in my face as she skidded to a halt. It was the announcement
our teacher had passed out two weeks earlier.

AMERICA'S GOT SCIENCE:
THE NEW GREATEST TV SHOW EVER!

**WORLD-FAMOUS SCIENTIST
PROFESSOR QUANDARY IS LOOKING FOR THE
COUNTRY'S GREATEST JUNIOR SCIENTISTS!**

COULD *YOU* BE ONE OF THEM?

**TEAM UP WITH A FRIEND* AND BRING YOUR
PROJECT OR EXPERIMENT TO TRYOUTS ON
SATURDAY, MAY 27! (NO SOLO ENTRIES, PLEASE.)**

TV CAMERAS WILL BE THERE TO WATCH PROFESSOR QUANDARY
HIMSELF PICK A WINNER FOR YOUR REGION, AND THE WINNING
TEAM WILL GO ON TO THE NATIONAL COMPETITION ON LIVE TV,
COMPETING FOR AMAZING PRIZES!

At the bottom there was a lot of small print spelling out
the rules and requirements and stuff.

"Three days!" Sam repeated, waving the colorful flyer

like a flag. She'd sprinted to catch up with me, but I noticed she wasn't breathing hard at all, and her dark brown skin wasn't even the tiniest bit sweaty from running. I might have been sweating, though. I could definitely feel my face turning pink. I always turned pink when I was under pressure.

"Sorry," I mumbled. "I forgot."

That wasn't true at all. I knew we were supposed to meet after class, only I'd been trying to skip. This project was going to be so much *work*, and I'd wanted one more day of freedom. One more day without being dragged through some boring experiment by Sam Baptiste, or writing out an official lab journal, or giving a presentation in front of TV cameras and hundreds of other kids and grown-ups and Professor Quandary and everybody. I just wanted the whole thing over with, and I figured the less time we spent working on it, the shorter it would be. I felt the same way about the contest as I felt about science and math class and school in general: blah, blah, blah.

Which was why it was the worst luck in the world that Sam and I were partners. Sam loved school. I mean, she *loved* it. Plus, Professor Quandary was basically her hero, so this contest was like Sam's personal dream come true.

And she wanted to win. Boy, she really, *really* wanted to win.

At first, I think she'd been just as unhappy about us working together as I was. But it seemed like not many people hung out with Sam, since she was the principal's kid and all. Plus all the other kids entering from our school already had partners, and the rules said we had to work in pairs.

I needed the extra credit. Sam needed a teammate. We were stuck with each other.

"Well," Sam said, putting the flyer back in her bag, "we're both here now, so let's see what we can do!" She sounded like her mom whenever I got sent to the office. "We agreed to have four more project ideas by today. Are yours ready?"

I shrugged and looked away.

"Billy . . ." Sam narrowed her eyes.

"Yeah, I guess," I said. Actually, I only had one idea, and Sam really wasn't going to like it. "But you go first."

"Okay!" Sam's frown flipped into a smile. She always smiled when she was talking about science. Or even just thinking about school. I didn't get her at all. "I thought it might be fun to test the chemical impact of salt water and chlorine on the plastic of different pool floaties!"

I shook my head. "I can't swim."

"Oh." Sam blinked, but her smile stayed on. "How about a pollution-absorbing paper that can be added to cardboard boxes to offset the impact of online shopping? Make them clean the air while they get shipped all over?"

"Cardboard makes me itch."

"No kidding. Well, my *favorite* idea was to design a deep-space telescope that can send greetings from Earth while it's busy looking and measuring." She grinned. "It would do multiple jobs at once!"

It was my turn to blink. Sam had been throwing complicated project ideas at me for two whole weeks. I'd shot them all down, figuring she'd run out of steam and finally suggest something easy, but that hadn't happened. Her ideas were still, like, high-school-level ambitious. I couldn't help feeling kind of impressed.

"Aren't telescopes sort of Professor Quandary's thing?" I said. "Didn't he invent one just like that?"

Sam made a disbelieving noise. "Professor Quandary invented the *Hyper-Quantum Telescope*, the one that let scientists finally see all the dark energy highways arcing between the stars. That's what made him famous and got him his weekly TV show. My telescope idea is *completely* different!"

"Oh. But okay, wait," I said, thinking fast. Designing a telescope sounded hard. "Isn't there kind of a risk people will still call us copycats?"

"Fine." Sam's eyebrows pressed together. "No telescopes.

But since you never, ever like any of my suggestions, why don't you tell me what brilliant ideas you've got?"

"Um, sure, yeah." I felt my face going pink again. I faked a cough. "I actually only have one idea today. I was thinking we could maybe do, you know, a sort of model volcano. You know, showing how they work? With, maybe, baking soda?"

Sam paused, letting her eyes go very wide. "A baking soda . . . volcano . . . That's your idea? Your *only* idea?"

Before I knew what was happening Sam had grabbed the top handle of my backpack and started pushing me down the street.

"Come on," she said. "That does it. We are going to your house right now, and I'm not leaving until we've got a *real* project idea and a plan to get it done. I am *not* losing this contest because of you, Billy Hamilton!"

I groaned, but I let her march me along. We did need *something* to present on Saturday, or I'd wind up the oldest kid in next year's fourth grade. It was a huge pain, sure, and it would definitely be super embarrassing standing in front of those TV cameras at tryouts. But it wasn't like it would be the end of the world or anything.

What was the worst that could happen?

CHAPTER TWO

(Sam)

"Hi, Mr. Hamilton!" I called as we stepped through Billy's front door.

I'd never been to Billy's house before—it wasn't like we were friends or anything—but I already knew his dad. Mr. Hamilton was on the PTA board with my mom, and I always helped out during their meetings. I knew he worked from home running his online party supply business and that he was big on hard work and responsibility.

I also knew I could count on him to put a little more pressure on Billy if he didn't start pulling his weight.

And Billy *had* to start pulling his weight. The entry form was crystal clear that teams had to decide on a project together, do the project together, and present the project together. Those were the rules. Set in stone. End of discussion.

Billy's dad came out of the next room as we were kicking off our shoes. Seeing the two of them side by side I realized they looked a lot alike, with the same freckly white skin and floppy brown hair. Although Mr. Hamilton's hair was, at my best scientific estimate, about 39 percent gone.

"Samantha!" he said, looking surprised. "Nice to see you. How's your mother?"

"She's fine, thank you."

"Please tell her I say hello."

"I will. Actually, may I use your phone? I need to tell her I'm here."

Mr. Hamilton led the way into the kitchen, which was neat and sunny and surgically clean. Billy trailed after us. I heard the two of them talking while I dialed my mom's office number.

"How was school?" Mr. Hamilton asked.

Billy mumbled something that sounded like "Okay, I guess," and Mr. Hamilton gave what was definitely a frustrated sigh.

But right then my mom answered and I missed the rest. When I put the phone back down the two Hamiltons were standing on opposite sides of the kitchen counter, not talking.

"My mom says to say hi, Mr. Hamilton," I said,

breaking the awkward silence. "And to thank you for having me over."

"It's our pleasure, Samantha. I imagine you're here to help Billy with some sort of schoolwork?"

I nodded. "We've got to finish deciding on our project for the *AMERICA'S GOT SCIENCE* contest."

Mr. Hamilton frowned. "Isn't that cutting it a little close? It's this weekend, right?"

I nodded again, shooting Billy a look.

"And don't you need the extra credit, Billy?"

Billy shoved his hands in his pockets. "We don't have to win or anything to get the extra credit," he said, speaking to the floor. "We just have to show up with a project."

Mr. Hamilton shook his head. "Barely meeting expectations again." He sighed. "Well, I suppose you can always do a baking soda volcano. You kids have fun." And he headed out of the kitchen.

I was so shocked I could have screamed.

What was wrong with everybody? There was no way something that simple would win us the contest and get us on national TV.

And what was Billy talking about? Of course we had to win! That was the whole point of entering! Professor Quandary, my absolute number one hero, was going to be in *my* town! In person! In three days! This was my chance to prove that *I* was the country's greatest junior scientist. And all anybody could talk about was baking soda volcanoes!

Mr. Hamilton's head popped back around the kitchen doorway. "Oh, by the way, if you kids need science supplies for whatever you decide to do, there might be some useful things in the attic."

"Huh?" Billy looked up. "There's science stuff in our attic?"

"Should be," said Mr. Hamilton. "My mom—your grandma—did science all through college, before she gave it up to do extreme sports." He wrinkled his forehead. "I never did find out why she did that."

"I'm sorry, but what?" I said.

"I know, right?" said Mr. Hamilton. "She was a very complicated person. Anyway, I came across her old trunks when I was moving some things around up there last summer. It's probably worth a look." He looked wistful for a second, patted the door frame, and disappeared.

"Why didn't you tell me your grandmother used to be a scientist?" I demanded as Billy led the way to the attic.

"I didn't know," Billy said. "I never even met her. She died the year I was born."

"I'm so sorry."

Billy shrugged.

The attic stairs were old and creaky, and when we got there and Billy turned on the lights I couldn't help whistling. Unlike the clean house and pristine kitchen, the attic was a total mess, dusty and crowded with boxes and crates and coatracks and other weird stuff. I suddenly wished I'd kept my shoes on.

"I guess we'll have to hunt around," said Billy. He sounded almost cheerful at the idea. "This'll be fun."

"If you say so," I said. I wasn't feeling cheerful. Getting our hands on some real scientific equipment would be great, but not if we had to dig through the Hamilton family's entire messy attic to find it.

Billy dove in enthusiastically but then got totally distracted by a garbage bag of novelty plastic nose-and-mustache glasses.

"These must be leftovers from my dad's business," he said after putting on a pair. His voice sounded funny. He made a muffled snorting noise. "Oh, that's why. The mustache is covering up the nose holes."

"The scientific term is *nostrils*," I reminded him, heaving aside an ancient set of suitcase-sized speakers.

"Sure, sure." Billy threw the glasses back in the bag and started flipping through an old knitting magazine.

I kept on looking, peering inside every box, crate, and container. Some had old blankets and clothes, but none of them had a single piece of useful scientific equipment. Until, finally, in the back corner, I came across a giant rusty green trunk and opened the lid.

"Hey! I found it!"

Billy crowded in beside me and we both stared with our mouths open. The trunk was crammed with beakers, test tubes, glass pipettes, and even a real old-fashioned microscope. Despite the dusty attic, everything was sparklingly clean and packed extra neatly. I had a feeling I would have liked Billy's grandma.

"Okay," Billy said, "that's actually kind of cool. Let's get it unloaded so we can see what we have."

I put out an arm. "We can't put all this clean equipment on the dusty ground!" I scanned the attic. "Here, let's use this."

I headed over to the wall, where a plastic kiddie pool was standing on its side. It was green with paintings of blue and yellow fish inside, and purple turtles dancing around the top.

"Hey, I remember that from when I was little," Billy said as I carried it over. "I wondered where it went."

With the pool shoved in beside the trunk we began unpacking the equipment, and the more we unpacked the happier I got. This really was professional-level science gear! Things I'd only ever seen in movies or on Professor Quandary's TV show!

Close to the bottom we found an old newspaper article set in a frame. It had a picture of a smiling young woman in a lab coat who looked a lot like Billy and his dad. A headline over the picture read *Local College Student Wins National Chemistry Prize.*

"Look!" I said. "Your grandma competed in science contests, just like us! And she won!"

"Great," grumbled Billy. "Another perfect Hamilton."

I ignored him and scanned the article. "She must have been a super-serious scientist to win a prize like this," I said. "I wonder why she gave it up. It says here she was only a year away from earning a double doctorate in chemistry and physics. That's so cool!"

"It definitely explains where my dad got his overachiever streak," muttered Billy.

I glanced over, curious, but he'd turned back to the trunk like he really didn't want to talk about what was bothering him. I didn't push.

Finally, the trunk was empty, and the kiddie pool was full.

"This is amazing," I said, looking over the treasure trove

of supplies. "But we've still got our main problem: What project are we going to do? This chemistry stuff would totally help if we did my pool floaty idea, only—hey, hello? Billy?"

Billy wasn't listening. He was peering into the empty trunk. He reached out a hand and tapped at the sides, then at the base.

"Billy?"

"Hey, pass me two of those glass jar things, will you?" he said. "Two the same size."

"They're called beakers," I said, handing them over. "And what for?"

"I want to check something."

Billy set one beaker inside the empty trunk, the other outside. He put a palm flat over the top of each one.

"Yes!" he said. "I thought so!"

"What?"

"The bottom of the trunk is higher than it should be." He leaned to the side so I could look. "See how my hands are at different heights? They should be about the same." He looked up, his eyes wide. "I think this trunk has a secret compartment."

It was my turn for wide eyes. "I thought you didn't like science," I said.

Billy made a face like he was being force-fed soap. "I don't."

"But you just did an experiment. You had a theory, you tested it, and you found an answer. That's science!"

"Nah." Billy was shaking his head. "Science is boring. I only noticed something weird and tried to figure it out."

"What do you think scientists do all day?" I said. But it wasn't the time for a lecture. Not when we had a secret compartment to open.

Using a metal spatula and pair of strong tweezers from the kiddie pool, we managed to get a grip on the bottom part of the trunk and pull. There was a creak, then a groan, and finally the whole thing lifted up. Billy had been right!

"I'll hold it open," I said. "You reach inside, quick!"

Billy stuck his hand underneath the panel and fumbled around.

"There's something here!" he said. "I can't . . . almost . . ." He reached in farther, biting his lip, then: "Yes!"

He pulled his hand back out, holding what looked like a stack of papers. I set the false bottom back into place, and as Billy held the bundle up to the light, I saw it wasn't just papers, it was . . .

"A book!"

"You don't have to yell," said Billy.

The book was old and had obviously seen a lot of use. There was a card set into a holder on the front. I shivered as we both leaned forward to read the words typed on it.

PRIVATE LAB BOOK OF

MARIANA HAMILTON

And underneath that, written by hand in big red letters:

TOP SECRET! DANGEROUS!
DO NOT TOUCH!

CHAPTER THREE

(Billy)

"Whoa!" I said.

"Whoa!" said Sam.

We both stared at the book in my hands. Why had my grandma hidden her top-secret personal lab notes?

"This is so amazing," said Sam, running a finger over the cracked brown cover. "If she hid this, it probably means it's got lots of advanced experiments inside! Maybe there's something in here we can do for the tryouts!"

Of course. Sam wanted to jump right in.

"I dunno," I said, trying to slow her down. "It says this stuff is dangerous. It's probably, you know, out of our league."

Sam gave me a look that reminded me of her mom again.

"Billy Hamilton," she said. "Are you saying I can't tell a

dangerous science experiment from a safe one? I am the most experienced scientist in our entire school."

"I know, but—"

"I understand the scientific method the way you understand breathing."

"Sure, only—"

"I would never do anything to put you, or me, or anyone else in danger."

"Okay, okay. I'm sorry."

Sam held out a hand, and I passed the book over.

"How are you even going to find anything good in there?" I asked as she flipped through it. "It'll take days to read it all." The book was seriously enormous, like someone had stuffed one handwritten textbook inside another.

But Sam was smiling.

"We don't have to read all of it," she said. "I'm guessing, from the way she packed her trunk, that your grandmother was a very organized scientist. And that means there should be . . ." She flipped to the front. "Yes! A key!"

I scooted so I could see over her shoulder. The key was neatly drawn in colored marker on the first page.

"Okay, it looks like your grandmother divided her research by substance," Sam said, flipping open to each section as she read. "See the color at the top of each page? The red section is for *Rocks & Gems*, blue for *Dusts & Powders*, yellow for *Light & Lasers*— Oh, that's weird."

"What?"

"The yellow section is missing."

Sam held the book up, showing a ragged gap between the pages that had blue bars across the top and ones that had purple. It looked like a whole chunk had been ripped out, right down to the binding.

"That *is* weird," I said.

"Extremely. But back to the key—purple is for *Gases & Vapors*, and green is for—"

Her fingers galloped through the pages.

"Bingo!" Sam slammed a finger down on the first page of the green section. In big block letters it read: *SLIMES*.

"Slimes?" I said.

"Slimes!" said Sam. She looked super excited. "You've made slime before, right?"

I nodded. "Who hasn't?"

"And it's pretty simple, right?"

"Uh-huh."

"Then you can't say no to this! All we need is a slime with a good enough twist to impress Professor Quandary. And if your grandmother thought they were worth writing down in here, they must be really, *really* good. Obviously she was totally brilliant!"

I chewed my lip. Slime *was* simple to make. And we could do it in time, unlike all of Sam's other wildly complicated ideas.

Maybe it was worth a shot.

"I guess you're right," I said.

"Of course I am!" Sam turned to the first page of the Slimes section. WORLD'S BOUNCIEST SLIME was written across the top. The rest of the page was written out almost like a recipe, with a list of ingredients and numbered steps describing the method. "See? Told you!" Sam grinned triumphantly.

A sputtering roar from out in the driveway made me look over at the attic window. That was my mom's motorcycle. She was home from work. The engine turned off, and I rolled my eyes as I heard the front door open and close. It would take a maximum of five minutes for Dad to tell her I was slacking on my science contest project. I could already hear the whole new lecture I'd be getting over dinner. Mom was a lawyer. She was good at lecturing.

My stomach clenched, and I turned back to Sam and the book. Who knew? Maybe Sam would find something that would actually get us somewhere in the tryouts.

For the first time in as long as I could remember I wanted to prove my parents wrong.

Sam was still flipping pages, muttering to herself. I just had time to read some of the titles: SILENT SLIME, WORLD'S WORST SLIME, SALTWATER SLIME, even one called POPCORN SLIME. Sam paused on that one, looking over the ingredients, then shook her head and moved on.

Finally, she slapped both hands onto the book and shouted, "Yes!"

I read the title between her fingers: WORLD'S MOST POWERFUL SLIME.

"This is perfect!" Sam said. Her eyes were flying from the page to the kiddie pool and back. "We have all the equipment we need right here. And the components . . ." She bit her lip. "Okay, some of them will be hard to get. But once we have them, we can make the slime no problem." She turned to me. "We can totally do this in time for the tryouts! What do you say?"

I knew she wasn't really asking. It was my fault we weren't done with a project already, and I'd already said I liked making slime. There was only one answer I could give.

I nodded, and Sam, smiling from ear to ear, shouted, "About time!" and high-fived me.

We had our project. It looked like I might pass fourth grade after all.

Before she left, Sam copied out the slime's ingredients, then divided the list in two.

Sam:

16 oz school glue

2 oz contact lens solution

8 oz black coffee

1/2 oz chalk powder

Billy:

32 oz pickle juice

2 oz sunflower petal paste

10 oz shaving cream

4 oz baking soda

"Okay," she said in full organizer mode. "So, let's both have our lists checked off by the end of school tomorrow. Then we'll meet back here to do the experiment. That'll give us until after school Friday to finish our lab notes, make a poster, and practice our presentation, and we'll be all set just in time for tryouts Saturday morning!"

I nodded. It was all I could do.

Sam Baptiste might be bossy, and she might be way too into science, but she sure did know how to get things done.

CHAPTER FOUR

(Sam)

By the time I got to school the next day I'd checked off almost my entire Slime-Component List, and I was feeling great. All I needed to finish it was a jumbo bottle of glue.

Luckily there are some serious perks to having your mom be the principal, and one of them was knowing how to get into the school supply closet. I'd wrestled a tiny bit with my conscience the night before—would helping myself count as stealing?—but then I figured that it was all for school anyway, since winning the contest would make my teachers look good.

I had to wait all the way until lunch to make my move, though, which made the morning totally drag. That was super weird. I usually loved every single second of class. Was this what school was like for Billy? Finally, the bell rang and everyone headed for the cafeteria.

I stood in line for the hot lunch, then ate as quickly as I could, going over my plans and dreaming of how great it was going to be when I won Professor Quandary's contest. I ate my lunch in the same spot as always, and the kids around me talked and shouted and ignored me as usual. That was fine. I didn't need them. They'd all want to be my friend and talk to me once I won the contest and became famous.

Billy was sitting in his normal spot at the end of the next table over. I'd noticed he never talked to anyone at lunch, either. *Hmm*, maybe we could start sitting together? I sat up tall and waved, but he didn't see me. He was too busy staring at the lunchroom monitors for some reason.

The girl sitting directly across from me stopped talking to her friend and gave me a weird look. I blinked at her, and her friend wrinkled her forehead and gave me a sarcastic little wave.

"Oh," I said, looking back and forth between them. "No, that wasn't— I didn't— Not you . . ."

They rolled their eyes in unison and went back to talking about soccer. I looked down at my tray and mushed what was left around with my fork.

As soon as the bell rang for recess I was up and out of there, feeling better with every step I took toward the office.

"Hi, Ms. Garcia," I said as I walked in.

My favorite school secretary smiled at me from the front desk. "Hello, Samantha! How's your day? I'm afraid your mother isn't in her office at the moment."

"Oh, that's too bad," I said. Actually, it was exactly what I'd been counting on. "Would it be okay if I ran in and left her a note? I just want to tell her I love her."

Ms. Garcia beamed at me. "Well, it's not strictly in keeping with the rules, but I don't see how your mother could mind," she said. And she waved me back.

I knew most kids were terrified of going to the principal's office, but for me it was one of the friendliest places in the school. Like most grown-ups, the secretaries were easy to talk to, and my mom was secretly super easygoing and the funniest person ever. It always made me laugh how stern she pretended to be in the halls.

Today her office felt even friendlier than normal, because the supply cupboard I needed was located right outside my mom's office door.

Since Ms. Garcia would be sure to mention my visit, I really did leave a note. I kept it short, just a quick *HI MOM I LOVE YOU!* on a Post-it on my mom's desk. I drew hearts around it just to be on the safe side, then slipped back into the office hall.

I looked around. No grown-ups. I could hear Ms. Garcia

talking on the phone at the front desk. I turned the handle on the supply cupboard, eased open the doors, and . . . bingo.

The cupboard was packed with school supplies: jars of safety scissors, rolls of butcher paper, stacks of Post-it notes, tubs of rubber bands, and, right there on the bottom shelf, giant jugs of school glue. I hugged one to my chest and eased the door closed.

Ms. Garcia was typing now. I could hear the clacking keys of her computer.

I tiptoed back into my mom's office and took a deep breath. This was the bit I'd been most worried about. I pulled her desk chair over to the window, climbed up on it, and let out a sigh of relief. I could reach the lock. As I carefully inched the window open, the noise and screams of all the other kids out at recess drifted in, along with the sudden tweeting of the playground teacher's whistle. Time was running out!

The jug of glue squeaked as I pushed it over the window frame and thudded as it landed in the bushes—the perfect hiding spot until I could fetch it after school. I closed and relocked the window, then pushed the chair back into place, feeling guilty and happy at the same time as I saw the big smiling picture of me my mom kept on her desk. I felt a little embarrassed, too. It was my school picture from the year before, and dang, third-grade me sure did love those hot-pink overalls.

"Thank you, Ms. Garcia," I called, giving her a wave as I left the front office.

"Anytime, dear," she said. "Don't be late back to class!"

I wanted to dance through the halls as I headed for my classroom. I'd gotten all my slime components! So long as Billy got his, everything was going to go okay. I couldn't wait to find out exactly what Mariana Hamilton meant when she said this slime was the WORLD'S MOST POWERFUL.

And hopefully I would find out very, very soon.

CHAPTER FIVE

(Billy)

"Billy! Billy Hamilton!"

I looked up from where I was waiting on the school's front steps and spotted Sam. For some reason she was running over from around the side of the building.

"I got all mine!" she declared as she reached me, waving her Slime-Ingredients List. There was a big check in every box, and her backpack looked extra bulky.

"Nice."

"How about you?" she asked.

Her eyes narrowed as I shook my head. "Billy . . ."

"I'm sorry!" I said. "I found the shaving cream and baking soda at home, but I haven't seen a single sunflower anywhere. And Ms. Wilson in the lunchroom got all suspicious when I asked her for pickle juice. She didn't believe me when I said it was for science. I know I probably should have snuck in the kitchen during recess or something, but I just couldn't. Ms. Wilson really scares me."

Sam's frown relaxed. "That's okay," she said. "She scares me, too."

"I thought nothing scared you."

"Missing my chance to impress Professor Quandary sure does! But okay, so we still need pickle juice and sunflower petals to smash into paste . . ." She thought, drumming her fingers on her list. "Well, I know where we can find the first one: at the grocery store."

"Sure, but I don't have any money," I pointed out.

"Neither do I," said Sam. "But I do have an idea."

The local EZ-Shop grocery store was only a few blocks from school, so we walked over. As soon as the doors slid shut behind us Sam marched straight up to an older lady in a red vest and name tag. The lady listened to Sam, then pointed, and before I knew what was happening we were standing in front of the long deli counter.

"Excuse me?" Sam called to a teenage boy slicing sandwich meats. He was as pale as the inside of a potato and had long black hair and a lip ring. From the look on his face he was about to die of boredom. "The manager lady up front said you might be able to help us. We need pickle juice for a school project. Do you have any extra?"

"Huh?" said the teenager. "Pickle juice?" Even his voice sounded like it was bored.

"Yes! You know, the stuff left in the jar after the pickles are gone?" Sam pointed to a big glass jar of pickles beside the deli cash register.

"Oh, pickle juice." The teenager's face didn't change. "Hang on."

He disappeared into the back room and returned with a jar the size of a Thanksgiving turkey. A red label on the front read INDUSTRIAL JUMBO PICKLES. Inside were at least two gallons of yellow-green liquid.

He pushed the jar over the counter. "Here."

"Thank you!" said Sam. "But we actually only need about four cups. Do you have a smaller jar we can use?"

"Nope," said the teenager. "All or nothing. Take it or leave it."

"We'll take it," Sam said. "Thanks."

The bored teenager shuffled back to his spot behind the sandwich meats and stood staring into space.

"That was like talking to a zombie!" Sam said under her breath. "Teenagers are so weird. But anyway, success! You grab the jar and let's go see if the floral department has any extra sunflowers."

"Why do I have to carry the jar?" I asked, pulling it into my arms. It was super heavy.

"Because I did all the talking to get it," said Sam cheerfully. "And pickle juice was on *your* half of the list."

I couldn't argue with that.

I tried to do more of the talking at the floral department, but the lady working there clearly wasn't into helping kids.

"No, we do not have any sunflowers today," she said, practically scolding us. "And even if we did, I wouldn't give them to you. Flowers cost money, children! People work for money, flowers cost money, so why should I give two children who don't work flowers for no money?"

I had a sudden great idea.

"Do you maybe have some old sunflowers nobody wants to buy?" I said. "They can be wilted or ugly-looking. We don't mind."

We could still hear the lady shouting as we made it through the sliding doors back to the sidewalk.

"I think you insulted her flower skills," said Sam.

"I was only trying to help," I said. "It's the very last ingredient . . ."

"Component," said Sam.

"Huh?"

"When something's in a food recipe, it's an ingredient,"

she said. "When it's in a scientific experiment, it's a *component*."

"Whatever." Sam might be really into knowing the right scientific words for things, but just thinking about it made my brain glaze over.

We started back. We were taking a different route from the way we came, looping around the other side of the school, and I wasn't paying much attention to our surroundings until Sam suddenly grabbed my arm.

"Hey, careful!" I said. "I almost dropped the jar!" But Sam wasn't listening.

"Look!" she said, jumping up and down and pointing. "Look! Look! Look!"

I looked, and saw a tiny house with a massive garden. The garden was full of flowers: purple roses, yellow lilies, and there, growing close to the sidewalk, a massive forest of sunflowers.

The whole thing would have been pretty, except for the black-and-red signs stapled one after the other all along the garden's white picket fence:

BEWARE OF DOG
NO TRESPASSING
PRIVATE PROPERTY

In a few spots a handwritten sign had been stapled in with the others, with three words scrawled in thick black marker:

KIDS KEEP OUT!

My blood went cold.

"Oh no," I said. "No, no, no. That's Mrs. Hubble's garden. We are *not* going in—"

But Sam was already crossing the street and jogging down the sidewalk. I sighed. The jar sloshed in my arms as I raced to catch up.

We stopped outside the fence. There was no sign of Mrs. Hubble. And no sign of her dog. Both of them were famous in the neighborhood. Most kids knew better than to even walk by her house. Even the mail carriers and package delivery trucks kept the engine running when they had to stop.

But she had sunflowers.

"Look at them," whispered Sam, staring longingly over the NO TRESPASSING signs. "Do you think Mrs. Hubble would let us have a couple if we knocked on her door and asked super, super nicely?"

"No!" I whisper-yelled. "You know the stories, right?

How she feeds all her plants a special fertilizer made of the ground-up bones of kids who've trespassed?"

"Those are baby stories," Sam said. "Besides, going up to knock on her front door isn't trespassing. We *need* those flowers for the contest! For Professor Quandary! What else are we going to do?"

Sam had been waving her hands as she talked, and as she finished she let her right hand rest lightly on the fence.

"No, stop!" I shouted. But it was already too late.

A huge, ferocious, ugly gray dog jumped up from where it had been sleeping under a rhododendron bush and came tearing across the perfect lawn, barking and growling. Sam jerked her hand back, but the dog kept coming, drool pouring from its mouth. It had almost reached us when the front door of the house opened with a bang and Mrs. Hubble appeared, looking just as gray, ferocious, and ugly as her dog.

"What's going on here?" she screeched. Her screech startled the dog, who tried to stop, but instead he tripped and skidded right through the patch of sunflowers, smacking into the fence with a crunch. Sam and I jumped back so far we were almost in the street.

"Gilbert!" Mrs. Hubble shouted as the dog scrambled to its feet. "Heel!"

Gilbert the dog heeled, trotting over to sit beside his owner. He was covered in dirt and still had drool pouring out of his mouth. His eyes narrowed and his ears went back as he glared at us. Mrs. Hubble was giving us the same look, hands planted on her hips, and the combination of the two of them, framed in the open door of the dark house, made my bones go cold.

"You! Children!" barked Mrs. Hubble. "What are you doing loitering outside my garden?"

I waited for Sam to answer, since she seemed better at talking to grown-ups than me, but she didn't.

I looked over. Sam wasn't at my side anymore.

"Down here!" came a whisper.

I couldn't see clearly around the pickle jar, but she was crouched low, doing something with her hands. "Keep her talking!" Sam hissed.

"I asked you a question!" screeched Mrs. Hubble. "And what is that girl doing down there out of sight?"

"She's, um . . . shoelace!" I called back. "She's tying her shoelace, ma'am. That's why we had to stop."

"Gilbert does not bark for shoelace tyers! You must have touched the fence, or been planning to harm my garden somehow! Which was it? And what's that jar of liquid you're holding?" Mrs. Hubble stabbed out an accusing finger, then gasped. "You were going to poison my garden, weren't you? Admit it, child!"

From somewhere around my feet Sam whispered, "Keep stalling!"

My mind was being battered back and forth like a tennis ball.

"No! We weren't going to poison your garden!" I said, my voice going all high. *Why weren't we just running for it? What was Sam doing?* "This jar is for an experiment. A science experiment. For school." Inspiration struck. "We're testing the kind of water flowers need to stay alive! And we saw your beautiful sunflowers, and we were wondering if . . . you know, if maybe we could—"

"Could what?" hollered Mrs. Hubble. "Spit it out!"

"Um, you know . . . have some?" I finished.

Mrs. Hubble's answer was like the lady from the floral department turned up to a hundred. She was only just getting started, screaming *How dare you!* and *I'll never part with a single leaf from this garden!* and *Thieves! Children and thieves!* when Sam jumped back to her feet. Without needing to say a single word, we both took off running, Gilbert's barks and Mrs. Hubble's screeches chasing after us on the air.

Two blocks later we felt safe enough to slow down.

"Well," said Sam, panting hard. "That . . . was . . . fun!"

"Fun?" The pickle jar was making my arms ache, and I was gasping for breath. "We didn't . . . get . . . even . . . one . . . single . . . sunflower!"

Sam stopped walking and turned to me with a massive grin. "Oh, didn't we?" And she pulled three rumpled, slightly squashed, but very yellow sunflowers out from under her T-shirt.

"What?!" I said. "How did you—? Isn't that—?"

"It doesn't count as stealing," Sam said. "They got poked through the fence when the dog ran into it. That means they were on the sidewalk, and the sidewalk is public property."

She looked super pleased with herself. And I had to admit, she had every right to.

"Way to go bending the rules," I said, giving her a thumbs-up.

"Thank you, I think?" Sam's smile twisted. "Anyway, this is awesome! We've got the last component!" She tucked a sunflower between my arms and the pickle jar, then held the others out in front of her like a torch. "Come on, Billy Hamilton. Let's go make some grand-prize slime!"

CHAPTER SIX

(Sam)

Billy's dad was walking by with a steaming mug of coffee as we lugged our gear through the Hamiltons' front door.

"What's all this?" he asked, eyeing Billy's sloshing jar of pickle juice and my crumpled sunflowers.

"Science supplies," said Billy. "For our project."

Mr. Hamilton frowned. "Those are some unusual science supplies. Well, don't make a mess, kids, and try not to blow up the house."

Up in the attic Billy groaned as he set down the pickle jar. "Look," he said, wiggling his arms like limp spaghetti. "Look how heavy that was!" He stopped and looked at me. "Hey, just so I'm clear. We *aren't* going to blow up the house, are we?"

I groaned, too, as I dropped my heavy backpack on top of

a chest of clothes. "No chance," I said. "We're going to follow your grandmother's lab notes exactly, and I didn't see anything in there that could cause a severe chemical reaction like that."

"You mean you understood the whole recipe?" Billy sounded impressed.

"The whole *method*," I corrected. "And, well, no, not all of it. It's complicated, for sure. Hopefully it'll make sense once we've done it."

"That's comforting," said Billy.

One of the big rules for Professor Quandary's contest was that we had to keep official lab notebooks as we went. That meant before we even got started mixing components Billy and I would have to write down what we were trying to do (our scientific objective), what we thought would happen (our hypothesis), and how we would do it (our method). When we were done, we would fill in our results.

OBJECTIVE: Create the WORLD'S MOST POWERFUL SLIME.

HYPOTHESIS: The WORLD'S MOST POWERFUL SLIME requires a certain complicated chemical reaction.

METHOD: Mix components together in the right order to cause reaction.

RESULTS: (pending)

"I'm so bo-ored!" said Billy before we'd even started copying down the method from his grandmother's top-secret lab book. "This is so much wo-ork. Why can't we just get on with mixing things?"

I did my best imitation of my mom's *stern principal* look.

"We have to do this right if we want to win on Saturday and get on national TV," I said. "And it makes sense to get our lab books done now instead of after. Once we've got a batch of the WORLD'S MOST POWERFUL SLIME to play with, you can bet we're gonna be totally distracted!"

I was trying to be nice. *I* could handle doing lab book work once the experiment was done, but I knew Billy Hamilton pretty well by now, and Billy Hamilton was going to be useless once he got his hands on that slime.

Billy slumped against his grandmother's trunk with a sigh so whiny it was almost funny.

"Okay, fine, we'll do the lab books," he said. "But for

all this work we better get on TV and win our million dollars."

My head shot up. "Win our *what*?"

"Our million dollars. I overheard some kid in the lunchroom yesterday saying the grand prize on *AMERICA'S GOT SCIENCE* is a million dollars each for the winning team."

I stared at him. As far as I knew the grand prize was a bunch of science books or a lifetime supply of beakers or something. Anyway, the real prize for me would be getting on the show and proving to Professor Quandary and the rest of the world that I was the greatest junior scientist in the country.

But if the idea of a million dollars was going to keep Billy working, I wasn't about to tell him otherwise.

"We'll do it," I said. "We'll get on the show and win all the prizes, but only if we get our lab journals filled out first."

Billy grumbled all the way through, but finally we were both finished and ready to start the experiment. It actually turned out to be a good thing we'd had to copy out the steps, since there were plenty of tricky bits we might have missed otherwise. The end result might only be slime, but we were about to do some really advanced science.

In other words: I was in heaven.

I looked over the components one more time, triple-checking that everything was laid out in the proper order.

"Ready?" I said to Billy.

"Sure, I guess."

I opened the bottle of school glue, and we finally—finally!—got our project underway.

According to the records I wrote in my lab journal, it took us exactly twenty-seven minutes to make the slime. But for me it felt more like twenty-seven seconds. Mariana Hamilton's instructions were a dream to follow, even through the tricky bits, and as we added the coffee, and the shaving cream, and somehow got the mashed sunflower petals to dissolve in the pickle juice, it was all the most fun I ever had in my life.

When it was over we sat there, kiddie pool filled with equipment on one side, leftover components on the other, one beaker of golden slime resting between us.

One beaker of glowing, golden slime.

One beaker of glowing, golden slime filling the dusty attic room with rainbows.

The light played over our faces as we both stared in silence. It was like something out of an alien movie.

Billy's mouth was hanging open. He looked like he was going to faint. Like his brain was absolutely refusing to believe that we'd made the thing sitting in the beaker in front of us.

My own brain was buzzing along at a hundred miles an hour. So many chemicals would have to be involved to make that kind of glow! Was it a similar reaction to the one deep-sea predators used to lure in prey? Or was it more like the kind happening in glowing fungi in some of the world's rain forests? Or what if this was some entirely new kind of phosphorescence? Some multi-prismatic enzyme that created light that automatically refracted into rainbows? Theories were speeding through my mind faster than I could think.

"It's so . . . beautiful," said Billy, his voice soft. Then, "I wonder what it feels like!" And before I could say a single word he grabbed the beaker and tipped the glowing slime out into his hand.

And the slime transformed.

The instant it met his fingers the slime *rippled*, like it was caught in an earthquake. The rainbow-reflecting sheen disappeared, and the substance started changing colors, like an octopus I saw once at the aquarium. Its glowing light went from gold to yellow green to red to purple, and finally settled into a swirl of luminous silver and blue.

"Wow!" said Billy. "This is so cool!" He squeezed the slime, moving it from one hand to the other. "It feels like air and water at the same time! Here, you try!"

He handed it over, and I gasped as the slime hit my fingers. It did feel like air and water! But it didn't change when I took it. It didn't ripple or shake, and it stayed the same glowing tie-dye of silver and blue.

"Why isn't it changing again?" Billy asked.

"I don't know." My mind was still racing. "Maybe it wasn't actually done when you touched it and the heat from your hands changed the recipe. Maybe this slime was never meant to be touched!"

"Well, that would be pointless," said Billy. "What's the use of slime if you can't play with it?"

"True," I said. "But *something* happened when you picked it up. Here." I handed it back over. "I have to get all this down in my lab book!"

I started scribbling notes on the glow and the color change that had happened, along with the slime's current texture, color, temperature, and consistency. The more data we had, the better my chances of figuring out what exactly we'd just created.

Billy finally had enough of squishing the slime from hand to hand and put it back in the beaker. It slowly settled in against the sides, the cool swirling colors pressing against the glass like miniature storms.

"It's weird, isn't it?" I said. For some reason I was keeping my voice down. "I still don't understand exactly what your grandmother meant when she named it, but this slime really does feel different somehow."

Billy nodded seriously. "I know what you mean," he said. "It's almost like . . . I mean, it almost looks . . ."

We both stared down at the beaker, saying the final word together:

"Alive."

CHAPTER SEVEN

(Billy)

I woke up to my alarm the next morning feeling better than I had in weeks. The weight of putting off the science project was gone! If I'd known it was gonna be this big a relief maybe I would have gotten started earlier.

All Sam and I had to do now was make our poster during school and throw together a presentation that night, and all the work would be done for the tryouts tomorrow. I'd be home free.

And until I left for school, I had the world's coolest slime to play with.

I hopped out of bed and headed for my desk, where the slime had spent the night in a Tupperware container. Sam had insisted on something airtight to keep the slime from drying out. I swear, she was treating it like an injured baby animal or something. The only reason I still had the slime at all was because she was scared of exposing it to different temperatures on the way back to her place.

But when I got to my desk I stopped so suddenly I stubbed my toe on my chair.

The Tupperware was gone.

And there was a stack of clean laundry in its place.

Oh no. Oh no no no no no.

My mom must have come in early with my laundry and taken the Tupperware to wash it. She had super-strict rules about dirty dishes in my room.

I was out the door and thumping down the stairs before you could count to three.

"Mom! Mom!" I burst into the kitchen and skidded to a stop. It was empty.

That was weird. Mom had to be up already, but it was too soon for her to have gone into work. And Dad was usually up by now, too, making coffee and listening to the news on the radio. Only they weren't there.

But the missing Tupperware was.

My heart catapulted up into my throat, then nose-dived down into my shoes. The Tupperware was sitting open in the sink. And it was very, very empty.

"MO-OO-OOOMM!" I yelled.

I bolted out of the kitchen and skidded to a stop in the living room. There was my mom, still in her bathrobe, staring out the window. I yelled her name again, but she didn't turn around until I tugged on her sleeve. The look on her face made me take a step back.

She was smiling, but not like an *oh good morning* smile. This smile was super wide, but it was faded, washed out, vacant. It was almost like she'd been smiling at an old memory and her face had gotten stuck.

"Mom?" I said.

"Oh, hello there," my mom said. Her voice sounded different. It was higher than usual, but also kind of husky around the edges.

"Are you . . . okay?" I asked. "Don't you need to get ready for work?"

"Work?" She said it like she'd never heard the word before. "Oh, no. I have work to do here."

"Um, okay." I was definitely weirded out, but I couldn't get sidetracked. "Mom, listen, this is super important. My science project was in the Tupperware that was on my desk. And now the Tupperware is in the sink. Did you— Did— Is the glowing stuff that was in there—" I took a deep breath. I almost didn't want to know. "Did you wash my slime down the drain?"

My mom's smile didn't change. Her eyes didn't blink. "Slime?" she said in her new dusky-sweet voice. "Drain?"

"Yes! Did you throw it out? Or did you save it somewhere?"

"Did I save what, honey?"

"My science slime!"

"Who?"

I was past worried now; I was frustrated. I just wanted to know! Why wasn't she telling me?

There was the sound of a door opening upstairs, and my mom turned her head to look. As she did, the light caught a streak of something shining across her cheek near her ear. Shining and silver and blue.

"You did get rid of it!" I said, pointing. She must have gotten an itch or something while she was emptying the Tupperware. "You've even got some on your face!"

"Hmm?" said my mom, turning back to me.

"Thanks for ruining everything, Mom!" I was almost yelling at her. Why couldn't she see what a big deal this was? Why couldn't she manage even a simple apology? And why wouldn't she stop that creepy smiling?

I marched for the stairs, trying not to think about how mad Sam was going to be.

"That's fine," I called over my shoulder. "Ruin my entire

life. And have fun working from home today, I guess. I have to go get ready for school. Not that it matters since I'm gonna fail fourth grade now and—"

"School?" interrupted my dad's voice.

He was coming down the stairs toward me. He was in his slippers and pajamas. His hair was a mess.

I backed up three steps at the sight of him.

He was smiling just like my mom.

"Yeah . . . school," I said. "Where I go every weekday?"

"Oh, no." My dad's voice had changed, too; it had gone sort of gurgly. Wet sounding. He crossed to the window and put his arm around my mom's shoulders. She leaned into him. "No school, honey."

I stared at them. My dad had never called me honey. Not once in my entire life. That was my mom's nickname for me.

And wait, hang on. Did my dad just say what I thought he said?

The best part of school might be the end of the day when the rules got flipped around, but this was different. This was too many things getting flipped around at once. This was chaos.

"So, Mom's not going to work," I said. "And I don't have to go to school today?"

My mom and dad shook their heads in perfect unison. "No school, honey," said my mom.

"No school," repeated my dad.

"But . . . I'm almost failing. If I don't keep up on my classwork—"

"We have work to do here," said my mom.

"Work here today," my dad said.

They turned their faces to smile at each other, and I saw a glimmer of slime shining on my dad's cheek. Gross! My mom must have smeared it on him during a hug or something. They were definitely being weirdly cuddly. What was going on with them this morning?

Whatever it was, stopping me from going to school was *extra* super weird. Not that they were really stopping me. I could always run out the door and go anyway if I wanted to. But going to school would mean facing Sam and telling her I'd lost our project. My stomach clenched just thinking about it. That would be the worst conversation ever. We didn't even have enough leftover ingredients—okay, *components*—to start over with a new batch.

Except, hey . . . we did have *some* supplies left. And if I was skipping school anyway, what if I used the time to try to do another of my grandma's experiments?

My stomach knotted again as I remembered how

complicated making the WORLD'S MOST POWERFUL SLIME had been, even with Sam there. Doing something from the book on my own was a serious long shot, but if I could pull it off, it might make up for losing the slime.

Maybe I could fix this.

I looked over at my parents, still smiling into each other's slime-stained faces, staring like they were counting eyelashes. They were breathing in perfect unison.

I didn't even bother saying goodbye. I ran out of the room and took the stairs two at a time to the attic.

CHAPTER EIGHT

(Sam)

Billy Hamilton's desk was empty.

I chewed my lip and stared at it as our class listened to the morning announcements. Maybe he was just late? Maybe he had a dentist appointment he forgot to mention? There was no way he would skip school. Not today. Not when he knew we were supposed to spend lunch and recess working on our poster.

Not when he knew we were almost out of time.

But Billy didn't show up by first recess. Or by the time class ended for lunch. His desk stayed empty, and after another awkward half hour of being ignored in the lunchroom, I went back to the classroom and did the work myself.

I got out the pens by myself, I measured the poster board by myself, and I filled in the full scientific description of the

WORLD'S MOST POWERFUL SLIME by myself, complete with side panels discussing different kinds of glowing and color-changing creatures.

Outside the window, kids were running and screaming on the blacktop, bouncing balls back and forth, laughing. It wasn't that I minded staying in from recess—no one ever talked to me out there, either—but maybe the noise of all those kids having fun wouldn't have sounded quite so loud if Billy were sitting beside me.

Someone knocked while I was coloring in a fluorescent jellyfish, and I looked up to see my mom standing in the open doorway, looking pretty like she always does. I'd already seen her fancy hair wrap and dangly silver earrings that morning at home, of course, but somehow her outfits always looked even more glamorous at school.

I felt my face light up. It was really good to see her.

"Hey, sweetie," she said, flashing me the secret family wave we used to say hi at school. "Staying in? Hard at work?"

"You bet!" I lifted the poster.

"Ooo! What a fun project! I'm so glad it worked out in time. Is Billy—" But whatever she was going to say next got cut off by the intercom.

"*Call for Principal Baptiste in the office. Principal Baptiste, please report to the office.*"

My mom sighed.

"Don't people know it's supposed to be my lunch, too?" She gave me a smile. "Bye, sweetie. I can't wait to see how your finished project turns out. Have an awesome rest of your day!"

She turned to go, and I had a sudden powerful urge to run over and squeeze her in a hug. But we didn't do that at school. That's what the secret family wave was for. I made the signal just in time for her to wink, and then she was gone.

I turned back to my jellyfish. One thing I knew for sure now: Whether Billy Hamilton was sick or not, I was heading over to his house the minute school got out, and he was going to help me finish this project. Because the clock was ticking, and there was no way in the world I was going to let myself, Professor Quandary, or my mom down.

CHAPTER NINE

(Billy)

By lunchtime, I was starting to think I would have been better off going to school after all. Sure, Sam would have yelled at me, and I'd be sitting at my desk feeling awful, but she was going to yell at me anyway when she found out the slime was gone. And at least at school I wouldn't have given myself such a massive headache.

My grandma's top-secret lab book had to weigh at least fifty pounds, but I'd dived right in, flipping through pages at random, looking for something, *anything*, that I could make. A lot of the experiments honestly went right over my head, but some I at least partly understood.

"Okay, these are pretty cool," I muttered to myself. "*Ultraviolet Rubies, Hyperactive Pollen . . . Fireproof Ice Cubes!*"

Of course, it turned out literally none of the cool-sounding ones were doable. Most of them had components that would be impossible to get—who has sulfuric acid just sitting around?—and the rest needed a blowtorch or electron microscope or deflector dish or something else I didn't have. So, it was back to square one.

When the headache started I put the book down on the floor so I could rub my eyes, and when I looked back it had flopped open to the gap where the yellow section used to be. The *Light & Lasers* section. The jagged edges of the missing pages poked out of the binding like a really bad haircut, with the last page of the blue *Dusts & Powders* section on the left, and the first page of the purple *Gases & Vapors* section on the right.

The first *Gases & Vapors* page was taken up with the section name in big block letters, just like the first page of *Slimes*, but . . . wait. There was something else there, too, just visible in the light coming in through the attic windows. It looked like words indented into the page. Lots of words. I leaned in to get a closer look.

Whatever my grandma wrote about on the last page of the missing yellow section, she must have been pretty excited. She'd really been pressing hard with her pen. Most of the indented words were unreadable, but I could just make out *dark*, and *quantum*, and *matter*, and *telescope*. The words *secret* and *research* showed up all over, and at the very bottom, in all caps and underlined about fifteen times, the word *BREAKTHROUGH*.

I frowned at the page, blinking. That all sounded like something to do with Professor Quandary's famous telescope Sam told me about, that Hyper-Quantum deal.

Why had my grandma written about it in her personal lab book? Was she just making notes on his discovery?

I shook my head, trying to sort it all out, and groaned. There was way too much stuff in my head already. I couldn't remember the last time I'd ever done this much work.

But I had to get back to it.

Before long, it became a struggle just keeping my eyes focused, even apart from the headache. My grandma's writing might have been neat, but it sure was tiny, and all the scientific names and terms and measurements began blurring together, like when you repeat a word so many times it becomes meaningless.

Just to make everything even more fun, my stomach had been growling from the minute I got to the attic, seeing as I'd skipped breakfast after the creepy encounter with my parents. Finally, I got too hungry to ignore it, slammed the book shut, and snuck back downstairs.

I found my mom and dad sitting at the dining room table. They were *still* smiling at each other. Empty soup bowls lined with green sludge sat in front of them, along with the plastic honey bear we normally only had out at breakfast.

"Oh, hello," said my dad.

My parents looked over at me. There were green smears around their mouths. Gross. It wasn't like either of them to make a mess when they ate.

"Get yourself some soup, honey," said my dad.

"We saved you a bowl."

The skin on the back of my neck prickled. They almost sounded like the bored teenager at the grocery store, the one who gave us the pickle juice. Talking like a zombie might be normal for teenagers, but it definitely wasn't for my mom and dad.

I went into the kitchen. A big pot sat on the stove, the biggest one we had. I grabbed a clean bowl and peered inside. There were green scum marks around the side almost all the way up to the top, but only a small layer of soup left at the bottom. It smelled bitter and kind of metallic. I scraped up what I could, suddenly wondering where the rest of the pot had gone. Had my parents seriously eaten everything else?

I returned to the table. My parents did look pretty full. They were both sagging back against their chairs. I sat down, took a spoonful of soup, put it in my mouth . . . and almost spat it right back out.

It was cold.

And not just room-temperature-cold, *cold*-cold. Something crunched between my teeth, and I spotted the melting remains of ice cubes hiding under the flecks of stringy green leaves in my bowl.

"What kind of soup is this?" I asked. Both my parents were way better cooks than this.

"Iced spinach," said my mom.

"Spinach, spinach, spinach," said my dad. "Here, add some honey, honey."

Before I could react he grabbed the honey bear off the table and added a thick squeeze to my soup.

"What do you think?" asked my mom. Her voice was even higher and raspier than before. She and my dad were staring at me intently.

I had no choice. I lifted a spoonful of icy, honey-covered spinach to my mouth. I chewed. It was the worst thing I'd ever tasted. My parents leaned forward, their creepy zombie smiles boring into me. I swallowed.

They relaxed, slumping against their chairs.

"All the soup is gone now," said my mom, letting her head tilt back so she was looking up at the ceiling.

"All the soup is gone," agreed my dad.

I sat there, waiting for something to happen. Was I excused now? Should I leave the table? I sure wasn't going to finish off this bowl of rancid evil.

My mom, still facing the ceiling, raised an arm and pointed at me. "You, honey," she said. "Buy more spinach for soup."

"We have work to do here," said my dad.

I stared at them. "You want me to go to the store?"

My mom nodded at the ceiling. Her creepy smile somehow got wider. "The store. Spinach for soup."

"Um, okay, I guess," I said. "But I don't have any money."

My mom pulled her wallet out of her pocket and handed me a stack of bills without looking. I took them and counted. I was holding one hundred dollars.

Whoa. It wasn't a million, but it was way closer than I'd ever been before.

"Lots of spinach, honey," said my mom. "You keep the change."

"Keep the change," my dad said. "Off you go."

"We have work to do here." They both pushed their chairs back and stood up, swaying. Without another word they shuffled out of the dining room. I heard my dad's office door close with a bang.

The table was still covered in their slimy green lunch

dishes. The kitchen was still a mess. Never once in my entire life had my parents not cleaned up after a meal. Being neat freaks was one of their favorite hobbies.

Something, I decided, as I snagged a granola bar from the cupboard and headed out the door with my pockets full of money, was very, very wrong.

CHAPTER TEN

(Sam)

Billy Hamilton was in big, big trouble.

Not only did he miss school the day before the tryouts, he wasn't even home when I got to his place to check on him.

And his dad wasn't helping the situation. Mr. Hamilton answered when I rang the bell, but when I asked if Billy was home sick he said, "Honey is getting more spinach, honey," shivered like someone had run a feather down his back, and closed the door in my face. Plus, he was smiling the whole time, and he had some sort of gunk in his ears.

Super weird. Super unhelpful.

I was pacing in front of their porch, trying to figure out what to do, when I spotted Billy himself coming up the street carrying two big paper grocery bags.

"Billy Hamilton!" I yelled. "You had better either be dying

of the flu or have a *really* good excuse for skipping out on school today and leaving me with all this work!" I waved the rolled-up poster I'd spent every second of my free time making.

Billy hurried over and dumped his bags down on the porch. Okay, more weirdness: From what I could see, they were full of plastic sacks of spinach.

"Wait, you really were buying spinach?" I said. "I thought your dad was joking."

Billy's eyes went huge. "You talked to my dad? Is he home? Is he still inside?"

"Of course he is. Isn't he always home? He answered the door and said you were out shopping."

Billy was clenching and unclenching his hands. "And did he seem . . . you know, normal?"

I rolled my eyes. "Apart from calling me *honey* and not letting me in? Yeah. Only no, wait, he had green stuff around his mouth and something near his ears. It looked like maybe food?"

"Yeah, okay, yes," said Billy. He looked terrified. "Still covered in soup, just like my mom."

"Your mom? Where's she?"

"She's at the grocery store," said Billy. "She stayed home from work today. She and my dad told me I wasn't allowed to go to school."

"Hang on, really?" I couldn't keep a little disbelief from creeping into my voice. I mean, PTA dad and lawyer mom told their kid to stay home from school?

"Really!" Billy said. "I swear! And then my mom sent me out to buy spinach after lunch. I had all this change she said I could keep—she gave me a hundred dollars!—but right when I was loading up on candy at the checkout I saw her coming in. She acted like she didn't even see me, even though she walked right past. And she still had soup all over her face. I was so scared I just bought the spinach and forgot the rest and ran straight back here."

I stared at him. I'd been expecting to find Billy home playing computer games or something. I never expected this.

"Okay, that's all super mysterious," I said, shaking my head. "But you and I need to focus on getting ready for the contest. How's our powerful slime doing?"

Billy looked scared then. Really, really scared. His pale face went as pink as my third-grade overalls.

"The slime . . ." he said, so soft I almost couldn't hear him. "The slime is . . . gone."

"WHAT?!"

He held both hands up in front of him. "I know, I know. I'm sorry! But it isn't my fault!" And he explained about waking up and finding the Tupperware empty in the sink.

". . . and I tried telling my mom how important it was, but I think she and my dad are doing some sort of marriage therapy or something? They're acting all weird and they won't stop smiling and I don't think they even care that our project is ruined. They just keep saying they have work to do."

"And so . . . do . . . we!" I said, bopping Billy with the rolled-up poster on every word. "Sorry your parents are acting strange, but there's nothing we can do about that. What we *can* do is finish our project, which is totally *not* ruined, so we can go on and *win . . . that . . . contest.*" I took a deep breath, pulling myself together. "All we have to do is calm down, focus, and make a new batch of slime."

"How?" moaned Billy. I thought he really might cry. "I spent all morning in the attic looking through my grandma's book. You know, to try to fix things? But I didn't find any other experiments we could do, and we used up most of the components we had yesterday."

I blinked. Billy had spent all morning reading his grandma's book? That was new. It was almost like he cared.

"That was yesterday," I said. "Today we can buy more components. You said you've got money now, right? The change from the hundred dollars? It's a good thing you didn't blow it on candy. We are going up to your attic, we're making a list of what supplies we need for another batch of

WORLD'S MOST POWERFUL SLIME, and we are going back to the EZ-Shop to buy it. Right now."

Billy still looked worried, but I could tell he knew I was right. Finally, he nodded and led the way into the house.

There was no sign of Billy's dad in the living room, but as we passed the closed door of the downstairs bathroom I heard glass clinking behind it, along with a murmuring voice that must have been Mr. Hamilton.

I tapped Billy on the shoulder. "Who's your dad talking to in there?"

Billy shook his head, his eyes wide and watery. "I don't have a clue what's going on around here anymore," he said. And even though I was still mad about the poster, I couldn't help feeling sorry for him.

We reached the attic. Billy opened the door, we stepped inside, and both of us gasped.

The kiddie pool was empty.

Every single piece of equipment, from the beakers to the microscope, was gone. So was the jar of leftover pickle juice, the spare sunflower, and all the other extra components, right down to the baking soda we'd spilled on the floor.

And so was Billy's grandma's super-top-secret lab book.

Footprints—big, grown-up footprints—led back and forth through the dust.

"It was here!" Billy said, stabbing both hands wildly at the kiddie pool. "It was all right here before I went down for lunch!" He stopped gesturing and clutched his face. "Oh no," he croaked. "My dad must have moved it. He must have taken it all while I was out at the store!"

Billy and I looked at each other. I could tell he was thinking the same thing I was. Piecing together data, coming to conclusions.

"Well," I said, "I guess now we know what's happening in your downstairs bathroom."

CHAPTER ELEVEN

(Billy)

"But why would my dad be doing science experiments in our bathroom?" I groaned, pressing my palms to my head like I could squeeze some sense out of the situation. "Why, why, why?"

Life was getting way too complicated. All I wanted to do was pass fourth grade and maybe win a million dollars on a science competition TV show. Was that so much to ask?

I flopped down cross-legged on the floor, not even caring that I was getting my pants all dusty.

"So weird," said Sam. "And why would he take the leftover pickle juice and everything, too? It makes no sense, unless . . ." She stopped, her eyes going super big.

"Unless what?"

She shook her head slowly. "Oh, no, I really hope I'm wrong. Come on, we need to get a closer look."

"A closer look at what?" I asked, but Sam was already heading for the stairs.

I clambered back to my feet and followed. She made a shushing sign as we reached the main stairs, and I tiptoed down after her, then along the hall and right up to the downstairs bathroom door. Sam pressed an ear to it.

"What's he saying?" I mouthed.

Sam frowned in concentration and shook her head. I pressed an ear to the door, too.

I could hear clinking bottles again—*our beakers*—and my dad's muffled voice. I pushed against the wood so hard I could hear my own heartbeat. A second later I thought my heart might stop as I finally made out what my dad was saying, over and over: "More slime, more slime, more, more, more. More slime, more slime, more, more, more."

"Oh, hello, honeys!" said a voice directly behind us.

Sam and I screamed and spun around.

My mom was standing over us, smiling, her arms full of bulging paper grocery bags. How had she snuck up like that?

"Oh, hi, Mrs. Hamilton," said Sam quickly. "Sorry, we were just, you know . . ."

"Yeah, Mom," I said. "We were only . . ."

My mom smiled down at us, swaying slightly. One of the paper bags had a tear on the bottom. The pointy orange caps of dozens of glue bottles peeked out.

My blood ran cold.

Sam and I pressed back against the door as my mom stepped forward. She leaned in close. "Hello, hello," she said in that new husky voice. "I have work to do."

She was so close now I could see that the blue-gray smear on her cheek hadn't dried. It was still glistening, and there was something else glistening, too . . . something shining . . . *inside her ear.*

"We'll get out of your way, then!" Sam gasped, and she grabbed me by the hand, yanking me toward the stairs.

For one terrifying moment I thought my mom might follow us, but she only kicked at the bathroom door with her foot. It opened, and I heard my dad say, "Hi, honey!"

My mom stepped into the bathroom, the door closed, and the lock clicked.

Sam and I shared one terrified look and raced back to the safety of the attic.

"Did you see those glue bottles?" gasped Sam, pacing back and forth, waving her hands in the air. "She must have bought out the store. They *are* making slime!"

"And she had *our* slime *in* her ears!" I was pacing, too. My heart was pounding.

"So our slime didn't just feel alive," said Sam. "It *was* alive!"

"And when my mom tried to throw it out this morning it climbed into her ears! And into her brain!"

"And she passed it to your dad and now it's making them act all weird!"

"And making them make more slime!"

"Probably so it can take over more people and turn them into . . . into . . . slime zombies, too!"

"Into *slimebies*!"

We stared at each other. Everything we were saying should have sounded ridiculous, but there was no other possible explanation. The WORLD'S MOST POWERFUL SLIME had taken over my parents.

This was really, really, *really*, really bad.

"What are we gonna do?" I whispered.

All at once Sam snapped her fingers. "Your grandma's lab book. There's gotta be something in there that can help us."

"But my parents stole it!"

"I know, but we copied down the experiment we did exactly," said Sam, diving for her lab book. "Maybe there's something we missed."

"World's most *powerful* slime?" I said. "World's most *dangerous* slime, more like!"

Sam was reading over the instructions again. "We did the experiment exactly right," she said. "The only thing your grandma doesn't mention is the bit where it changed color when you touched it. There's nothing about that in here."

I frowned. "So, maybe it is heat activated, then? Maybe that brings it to life? Only why wouldn't it say that in the book? If the slime can take people over, why wouldn't my grandma leave some kind of warning?"

Sam snapped her lab book shut. "Well, she sort of did," she said. "Remember the front cover? TOP SECRET! DANGEROUS! DO NOT TOUCH!"

"Oh, like that would ever stop anybody!" I kicked at my grandma's empty trunk in frustration. A thump and the sharp tinkle of breaking glass came from inside.

Sam's head whipped up. "What was that?"

I peered in and saw the framed story about my grandma. I'd propped it back inside the trunk for safety, and it looked like my slimebie dad hadn't wanted it.

"Whoops," I said. "I knocked over the newspaper article. Broke the glass. Sorry, Grandma."

"Don't cut yourself," Sam said as I reached in to get it.

She opened her lab book again with a sigh. "There just *has* to be something here that can help us . . ."

But while she was flipping pages and grumbling, I was busy staring at one corner of the article. The broken glass had torn the thin newsprint, and something colorful was poking through underneath. Something shiny.

CHAPTER TWELVE

(Sam)

"What's up?" I asked. Billy was poking at the broken picture frame, sticking his tongue between his teeth like a concentrating toddler.

"There's something else here."

I heard the scrape of glass shards, then the crinkle of newspaper.

Billy's face went green.

"Sam," he said. His voice was all squeaky. "Sam, Sam, Sam!"

I scrambled over. "What? What? What?"

Wordlessly, Billy held out the frame.

It turned out the article had been covering a glossy photograph. The photo showed two smiling people standing in front of a table covered in scientific equipment. They were both wearing lab coats and goggles. The person on the left had to be Mariana Hamilton. She had Billy's smile, his dad's ears, and a swoopy, shaggy haircut I remembered seeing on a '90s sitcom my mom still watched sometimes.

I recognized the person on the right, too, but in a way that made my stomach flip over and my head spin. Especially since the word *LIAR* was scrawled across his chest in thick black marker.

It was Professor Quandary.

"What?!" I said, grabbing the frame.

"I know!" said Billy.

I stared. Professor Quandary looked way younger, but it was definitely him. It was the famous face from TV, the face from all the books and posters and the *AMERICA'S GOT SCIENCE* tryout flyer. The same charming smile, same floof of hair, everything.

"Your grandma *knew* Professor Quandary?" I said, still barely believing what I was seeing.

"I guess so," said Billy.

"But he's my favorite celebrity in the world! Why didn't you tell me?"

"Hey, I didn't even know my grandma was a scientist until the day before yesterday, remember?" Billy said. "Anyway, it looks like she didn't like him very much."

I ran my finger over the word *LIAR*. "You're right. But she must have liked him enough *sometime* to smile for this photo and then put it in a frame. They look like lab partners here; I wonder what happened."

Judging by the mess in the background, the photo of the smiling lab partners had been taken right in the middle of an experiment. There were test tubes, vials, scales, beakers, even the microscope Billy and I had found in the trunk, plus components: bottles, powders, a jar of pale green liquid, a can of shaving cream, an open box of baking soda . . .

"Wait," I said. I held the picture right up to my nose. Was that spot of yellow a sunflower petal? "Wait, I think . . . maybe . . . *no* . . . but yeah! It has to be!"

"Has to be what?" Billy pushed in beside me.

"All the stuff on the lab table: coffee, school glue, *pickle juice*! Billy, I think your grandma and Professor Quandary were working on the WORLD'S MOST POWERFUL SLIME when this photo was taken!"

We looked at each other, our eyes wide.

"So, either they never found out it can activate and take people over . . ." I said.

"Or they did find out and somehow fixed it," Billy finished.

I whistled. If she'd lived through this slimebie business before, it was a real shame Mariana Hamilton wasn't still around to help us.

"I wonder if that's what caused their split," I said, looking back at the word scrawled across young Professor Quandary. "Maybe he suspected the slime might be dangerous and didn't warn your grandma? We know for sure he was a better scientist, since he invented the Hyper-Quantum Telescope and become famous, and she, you know, gave it all up. Maybe—"

"Telescope!" Billy's yelp was so high he sounded like a squeaky dog toy. "Liar! I—I just remembered . . . and maybe . . . but it couldn't really . . . No! He wouldn't . . . Or do you think?"

"Billy?" I said, using my mom's calm grown-up voice. "I'm gonna need you to finish at least one sentence if you want my opinion on something. Especially right after interrupting me."

"I'm sorry, I just . . . There's something I found earlier, before, in my grandma's lab book. Something I never told you. And I think it might change everything."

When Billy was done explaining, I could only sit there, staring at him.

"Let me get this straight," I said, trying to piece it all

together. "You found a few random words indented from the last page of the missing yellow section, and you think it proves something?"

"Not random words!" Billy's eyes were bigger than I'd ever seen them. "It was words like *dark*, *quantum*, *secret*, and *telescope*!"

"And you're saying those words, combined with this photo, mean . . . no. No, I can't believe it."

"Look at the evidence!" said Billy. He was raising his voice now. "You said yourself the stuff in my grandma's lab book was brilliant. That means the *Light and Lasers* section must have been brilliant, too. And it doesn't make sense that *she'd* tear it all out, does it? But someone sure did.

"Now we've got this photo that proves she was working with Professor Quandary, and she says he lied to her about something important. And sometime after this photo was taken, he became this big famous expert on light and lasers and telescopes, the same stuff we *know* my grandma was writing about that went missing. Even using the very same words!"

He let out a big breath. "Sam, I think the data is clear: Professor Quandary stole the plans for the Hyper-Quantum Telescope from my grandma. His whole career is based on a lie."

My brain heaved up and down like the worst ride at a fair.

I didn't want to believe it. I didn't even want to hear it. But Billy did have a point. He was turning into a real scientist whether he wanted to or not, and the data he'd presented did look at least a little bad for my hero, my science idol, my role model.

Only I couldn't accept such a terrible thing. Not just like that. I had to believe this was all just a mix-up. All a mistake. I had to give Professor Quandary the benefit of the doubt.

I was just opening my mouth to say something, anything, when the doorbell rang downstairs.

"Who . . . ?" said Billy, his head snapping up. I frowned at the open attic door, trying to refocus on the serious problems we were dealing with right there in the house. The doorbell rang again.

Why weren't Billy's parents answering it?

Billy and I looked at each other, and after a moment I nodded. We got up and tiptoed carefully down the stairs, stopping where we'd have a view of the entryway.

The bell rang again.

"I guess maybe *we* should get it?" whispered Billy. He sounded scared, and I didn't blame him.

The bell began ringing nonstop as we reached the door.

Billy turned the lock, then the handle, and peered cautiously through the crack . . .

. . . just as a sneaker-covered foot slammed into the door from the outside, flinging it wide and sending both of us sprawling to the ground.

CHAPTER THIRTEEN

(Sam)

Three grown-ups were squeezed together on the porch.

In front was a short middle-aged lady with light brown skin, a graying ponytail, and one foot still in the air from kicking the door open. At first I couldn't place why she looked familiar, then it clicked. This was the manager of the EZ-Shop, the one I'd asked for directions to the deli counter. She had a bulging bag from the store swinging at her side, and as the sun caught it I saw it was full of cans of shaving cream.

The second person was from the EZ-Shop, too: the angry white lady from the floral department. She was hugging a jumbo jar of pickle juice just like ours, although hers still had all the pickles in it. There were veins standing out on her arms and sweat dripping down her forehead.

The third person was hidden by the first two. All I could see was a gray bun over the florist lady's shoulder.

"Can—can I help you?" said Billy. Neither of us made any move to get to our feet. The ladies in front were smiling just like Billy's mom and dad. And even from here we could see the terrible truth: their ears were glowing and pulsing with slime.

"Oh, hello," the three of them said. Their voices were all different—high and screechy, low and buzzy, wet and gurgly—and together they made fingers walk up my back.

"We have work to do," said the EZ-Shop manager.

The door to Billy's downstairs bathroom flew open behind us. His mom stepped out.

"Work to do!" she said, smiling at the visitors.

"More, more, more," croaked the angry florist.

Billy's mom swayed back into the bathroom, and the trio on the porch trooped inside, walking right past Billy and me, heading after her.

As the manager and florist passed, we finally got a clear look at the person in back, and I got a jolt like my entire body had been plugged into a light socket: It was Mrs. Hubble.

Mrs. Hubble was always scary, but now she'd become absolutely terrifying. Her sagging frown lines were all stretched and warped by her wide slimebie smile. Slime oozed around the edges of her hearing aids. Worst of all were her hands, which were caked in dirt and clutched, like rotten tree roots, around a massive armful of sunflowers.

It looked like every single sunflower from her garden, pulled up one by one by the roots.

Billy gave a sort of mini scream as she stepped inside his house, scattering dirt all over the floor. I couldn't blame him. If the slime was powerful enough to make Mrs. Hubble rip up her own flowers, then it was powerful enough to make her do anything!

Mrs. Hubble stopped walking and looked down at us. Slowly, so slowly, she leaned over. The sunflowers smelled good, but not good enough to cover the stench of Mrs. Hubble's breath. Her eyes looked out of focus, but they still managed to pin us to the floor like bugs.

"Oh, hello, honeys," she said. Her voice was the worst yet, like centipedes crawling down the inside of a gym sock.

A new fear suddenly gripped me. Was Mrs. Hubble powerful enough to turn Billy and me into slimebies, too? Was the only reason we'd escaped so far because deep down all the other slimebies liked kids? Were we doomed now that she was here?

Mrs. Hubble got so close I could see the slime in her ears pulsing like a heartbeat. I had a wild urge to try to rip it out and stomp on it. But would that even help? Probably not. The slime probably went all the way to Mrs. Hubble's brain, and I couldn't dig that far.

Beside me Billy had a hand over his mouth to keep from screaming again.

"More, more, more!" gurgled Mrs. Hubble, her smile folding in around itself. Then she straightened up, her sunflowers swaying, and followed the others to the bathroom. The door snapped shut behind her.

Billy and I stayed right there on the floor, frozen, listening to the chanting voices, the clink of bottles, and the faint sound of tearing petals.

It was a miracle we didn't just run away right then and never look back.

Instead we got to our feet, closed the front door, and climbed back to the safety of the attic, which was starting to feel like our own secret hideout.

"What are we gonna do? What are we gonna do? What are we gonna do?" Billy moaned. He was pacing and so freaked out he almost fell into the empty kiddie pool. "My mom must have spread the slime when she went to the grocery store, and those new slimebies must have passed it to Mrs. Hubble on the way here! And did you see all those supplies they brought? They're making a huge new batch of slime! And what's gonna happen when it's done?"

"This is so, so serious," I said. I was pacing again, too. "Although, at least *we're* safe. I was certain we were gonna get slimebied by Mrs. Hubble, but it looks like the slime doesn't try to take over kids. I wish I had a scientific clue why not."

"Does it really matter?" said Billy. "If the slime keeps spreading we're gonna have extra-major problems soon anyway. Who's supposed to, you know, cook and drive cars and go to work and stuff if everyone except kids gets turned into slimebies? Who's gonna run things?" He linked his hands behind his neck and looked up at the ceiling. "I never, ever thought I'd say this, but we've gotta find a way to keep the grown-ups around."

"Hey, most grown-ups are pretty cool, you know," I pointed out.

"And you," said Billy, dropping his arms, "are such a principal's kid."

"Thanks!"

Billy smiled with one side of his mouth. "Back to our problem, we should try to get at least one grown-up on our side, right? To help us save the others? Only I can't think of any grown-ups who would even believe us. This is all way too weird."

He was right. My mom might be the coolest, but I knew she would never believe our science project was turning people into zombies. Not without seeing it with her own eyes, at least. And that would just get her slimebied.

But wait, if all we needed was a grown-up who would believe us without having to *see* the slimebies, what about—

"Professor Quandary!" I shouted.

"What?"

"Professor Quandary! He's a grown-up! And this proves he already knows about the slime." I scrambled for the picture and held it up. "He probably knows plenty of things we don't! And he's coming into town tomorrow! We can ask *him*!"

"Are you serious?" Billy said. "Don't you remember what my grandma wrote on his picture? And how would we even get to talk to him? Or are you saying we should just shout questions at him during the tryouts?"

"Don't be ridiculous," I said. "We can catch him before the tryouts. His flight from Chicago lands at 8:55 a.m., and he's taking a cab straight to the Conference Center where they're being held. That's a half hour drive from the airport, so if you and I are waiting out front on the sidewalk by 9:30 we should get our chance."

Billy was staring at me.

"What?" I said.

"How on earth do you know all that?"

"All what?"

"That!" Billy flapped a hand. "How do you know Professor Quandary is coming from Chicago, and that his flight lands at 8:55, and that he's taking a cab straight to the Conference Center?"

"Oh. Well, I mean . . ." I felt myself blushing the tiniest bit. "He is—*was*—kind of my biggest hero in the world. When I heard he was coming to town I made sure to find out his exact schedule in case I could manage to, you know, bump into him somewhere."

Billy laughed, but not in a mean way. "Nice going. So, our plan is to run up to Professor Quandary tomorrow morning, tell him about the slimebie problem, and hope he knows a way to help?"

"Yup. Pretty much. And I know your grandma said he's a liar and you think he cheated her, but I really can't think of a better option."

"Me neither. Let's do it."

"Let's do it," I repeated. I took a deep breath and let it out. We had a plan. Everything would be okay.

"So, what now?" asked Billy.

I checked my watch. "It's getting late. I really should head home to help make dinner. Plus, I want to make sure my mom stays inside and doesn't get slimebified. Think you'll be okay here?"

Billy bit his lip, then nodded. "I'll be fine. It's not like the slimebies are gonna try to eat my brains or rip off my ears or anything. They're just making batches of super-slime in our bathroom." His eyes got wide. "But hey, wait, slime! Tomorrow! The tryouts! What are we going to present?"

I almost laughed. It was hilarious to see Billy suddenly so worried about the contest.

"I already thought of that," I said. "We have to get your parents and the other slimebies back to normal first, but once we do, all the slime they're making now will be up for grabs. It should be identical to the batch we made before, all glowy and stuff, remember? So that's what we'll bring to the tryouts. In a sealed container, obviously!"

"But won't Professor Quandary know what it is?" asked Billy.

"Totally. Which means he'll know we did, like, college-level chemistry! He has to be impressed by that! It's not like he can disqualify us just because it's dangerous."

"He better not," Billy said. He took his grandma's picture from me and narrowed his eyes. "And if he tries, I'll ask him right in front of everybody exactly where he got the idea for his world-famous telescope."

Billy insisted on walking me to the door. We tried to be extra quiet going past the slimebies, but there was so much noise coming from the locked bathroom it didn't matter anyway.

"I'll come get you at nine tomorrow morning," I said out on the porch. "That'll give us enough time to walk to the Conference Center. It's only a mile away."

"Cool," said Billy. "Thanks." He looked back over his shoulder into the house. He seemed nervous.

"Are you sure you don't want to stay over at my place tonight?" I asked. "I think I could talk my mom into it. And I only live a few streets away."

Billy shook his head. "No, thanks. I need to stay here and look after my parents. You know, in case they do something really dangerous without meaning to."

"Well, just don't have slime in your ears when I come get you in the morning."

"Ha!" Billy's laugh was awkward. "I won't."

We waved goodbye, and the last I saw of him before the door closed was the smile dropping from his face.

My stomach twisted as I walked. Poor Billy. I really hoped he was going to be okay. I'd gotten kind of used to having him around over the last couple days. It was nice having someone to bounce ideas off. Someone to tackle problems with. Even someone to get yelled at by weird grown-ups with.

I stopped dead. Wait. Was Billy Hamilton my . . . friend?

My brain skimmed over the data, analyzing evidence and cross-checking patterns.

Whoa. I never would have believed it, but a good scientist doesn't ignore results just because they're unexpected. The results were in.

And the answer, at least from my side of things, was yes.

CHAPTER FOURTEEN

(Billy)

After Sam left, I stayed in my room with the door half open, trying to keep an ear out for what the slimebies were up to. It was weird. I always hung out in my room on my own, but right then it felt kind of lonely. I guess I'd gotten used to having Sam around to argue with.

Nothing happened for about an hour, but then I heard the creak of the bathroom door and thumping feet. I snuck down just far enough to watch the angry florist, the grocery store manager, and Mrs. Hubble leaving through the front door. They all had the same big smiles. They were all empty-handed.

At first I was relieved—those weird grown-ups were out of my house! Then I realized that meant three slimebies were wandering the neighborhood. Were they just heading out for more slime supplies? Or was their mission to make more slimebies? Maybe I should have tried to barricade them in somehow.

My mom and dad were still shut up in the bathroom, so I made myself dinner from what I could find in the kitchen. I was just adding my dishes to all the spinachy bowls in the sink when the doorbell rang. And rang and rang and rang.

The slimebies were back.

The slime must have been learning because this time my mom answered the door. I watched from around the corner of the kitchen as Mrs. Hubble marched in, bringing *three new slimebies* with her. That made, what, eight now? More, probably, since the florist lady and manager were still out there. How far could this thing spread?

Mrs. Hubble and the new slimebies swapped the usual greetings with my mom: "Oh, hello," "We have work to do," "More, more, more!" then followed her into the bathroom.

I sprinted back upstairs, fighting down a shiver. The slime problem was getting worse, maybe much worse. But for right now, there was nothing I could do to stop it.

The doorbell rang so many times that night I stopped counting. I stayed in my room, not even watching to see who'd been slimebified anymore. What was the point?

Somehow I fell asleep, even with all my lights on. I woke up suddenly around midnight, so thirsty I thought I was going to die.

I sat up, listening carefully. At first the house seemed silent, but then I heard a faint crunching sound from downstairs, like boots in week-old slush. It made the back of my neck prickle.

I had to see what was going on.

My bedroom light spilled onto the landing as I eased my door open and peered out. The rest of the upstairs was dark. The stairs were dark. The crunching sound was louder.

I tiptoed into the upstairs bathroom and drank two glasses of water as fast as I could. Then I went back out on the landing.

What were the slimebies doing down there? What was that sound? And why was it making me so queasy?

I started walking downstairs extra, extra slowly, shifting my weight on each step. Who knew what slimebies did at night? Maybe they changed shape, like werewolves at the full moon. Maybe they started going after kids. Maybe I was in serious danger.

I reached the bottom of the stairs . . .

. . . and swallowed a scream.

My house was overrun with slimebies. Dozens and dozens

of smiling, swaying, slime-controlled bodies. It looked like half the neighborhood was there. More slimebies than I'd ever imagined. *Way* more than Sam and I could ever deal with, even if Professor Quandary did manage to help.

They were packed in shoulder to shoulder, squeezed together like too many crayons in one box.

And they were feeding.

Every single one of them was gorging on icy spinach-honey soup. They were slurping it out of bowls, licking it off plates, tipping their heads back to pour it out of mugs. I could hear the crunching ice and the spinach leaves squishing between their teeth. Their lips smacked with sticky honey. The soup was getting all over their faces, all down their fronts, all over the walls, the floor, everywhere.

There was a clang from the direction of the kitchen, and I watched, feeling completely sick, as my dad pushed through the crowd, carrying a pot of what was clearly more soup. The slimebies dipped their cups and bowls and plates into the pot as he edged slowly through the crowd. Mrs. Hubble even reached right in with her wrinkly hands. By the time my dad had circled the room once, the pot was empty, and he disappeared back into the kitchen.

It was a nightmare. The slimebies looked like one giant, swaying monster with dozens of desperate, smiling mouths.

It was way too easy to picture them coming after me next, pulling me apart piece by piece and slurping me down for dessert, licking their fingers after.

I was so scared I thought I might throw up. I ran back upstairs, my teeth chattering, and shoved my desk in front of my bedroom door.

I stretched out on top of my covers again, but there was no way I was getting back to sleep. There was a whole army of slimebies filling the house beneath me, and as I lay there, staring up at the ceiling while the slow minutes turned to hours, I could still hear the sound of their chewing.

It was the worst night of my entire life.

CHAPTER FIFTEEN

(Sam)

I got the best sleep of my entire life that night and woke up extra early Saturday morning to get ready. Finally, it was tryouts day!

And okay, sure, there was a slime-zombie invasion going on. And my absolute hero, Professor Quandary, might actually be a massive thieving fraud. But these tryouts were still going to be the most important thing that had ever happened to me. This was my best shot to show the world exactly how serious a junior scientist I was. And nothing was going to stop me from taking it.

I studied my closet for a long time before picking out black dress pants, my favorite teal button-up shirt with science equations all over it, the white lab coat my mom gave me for my last birthday, and my best pair of comfortable white sneakers. Other kids would probably be wearing fancy dress shoes, but I knew real scientists spent a lot of time on their feet, and comfort mattered.

"Ooh, nice outfit, sweetie!" said my mom when I walked into the kitchen. She was still in her bathrobe. "But don't you want to save your nice clothes for after breakfast?"

"No time for breakfast, Mom," I said. "I'm heading out. I'm meeting Billy at his house at nine."

"But what about Saturday waffles?" My mom looked hurt. "I bought strawberries!"

My stomach rumbled. I really, really wished I could stay. Saturday morning waffles were a tradition for us. No one at school would ever believe it, but my mom the principal had a real sweet tooth and could totally let loose when it came to whipped cream, syrup, and strawberries. She'd even made up a dance specifically for using the waffle maker.

But I'd just have to miss it this week. Billy and I *had* to get to Professor Quandary before he got slimebied. And anyway, I wanted to make sure Billy was okay after spending the night in his house of weirdness!

"Sorry," I said. "I'm, uh, too nervous about the tryouts to eat." It wasn't a lie; I *was* nervous. "And Billy and I still have to practice our presentation some more!" Okay, that part was kind of a lie, but a tiny one.

"Well, okay, sweetie, it's up to you," said my mom. "Go get your presentation polished, and I'll drive the two of you to the Conference Center later."

"I think we're going to walk, if that's okay?" I said quickly. "We're getting there early to help set up."

My mom frowned a little. "Are Billy's parents going with you?"

I really hope not! I thought, but I crossed my fingers behind my back and nodded. I felt bad not being honest with my mom, but it was for her own safety. I had to keep her away from the Conference Center until we had the slimebie situation fixed! I left to the sound of batter sizzling on the hot waffle maker, my stomach still growling.

I only had to walk a couple streets, but I was seriously weirded out by the time I got to Billy's place. It was Saturday morning. There should have been people out getting the paper, or jogging, or even washing their cars already. But the streets I passed were almost silent. I spotted a few kids playing in their front yards and one or two confused-looking teenagers peering out of windows, but that was it. Where were all the grown-ups?

I found Billy sitting on his front porch. He had dark circles under his eyes.

"Are you okay?" I asked, running up to him. "Why are you out here?"

"I'm fine." Billy got to his feet. "It's just way more crowded inside than it was yesterday."

"What do you mean?"

"See for yourself."

We walked around the side of the house. I had to hold back a gasp when I saw the view through his dining room window. The place was jam-packed with grown-ups. They were standing squished in together, shoulder to shoulder. And they were all talking. I could hear the rumble of voices through the glass.

"They just kept showing up yesterday," Billy said. "And then they had this midnight spinach soup party." He shuddered. "And when I tried to come downstairs this morning they were all crowded together like that, smiling and chanting these three words over and over. I had to use the tree outside my window to get out here."

"What are they chanting?" I asked. I couldn't look away from the swaying mass of grown-ups. They looked almost like the arms of a monster sea anemone, all waving in an underwater current.

"*Find what's missing*," said Billy. He shuddered again. "It's like there's one voice speaking through them. It's horrible."

"*Find what's missing?*" I repeated. "But that makes it sound like something's going wrong with their new slime. Like they can't find a component or something. That's great! We might really stand a chance now. Especially if all the slimebies are staying put in your house."

Billy shook his head. "Not all of them are. Five of them left. I saw from my bedroom window. Maybe to find whatever they're missing?"

"When?"

"I think like an hour ago?"

"That means they could be anywhere," I said. I checked my watch. "Well, come on, it's a race now. We've got to get to Professor Quandary. Hopefully we'll find our answers before this slimebie army finds theirs!"

CHAPTER SIXTEEN

(Billy)

The Conference Center was located on the outer edge of the next neighborhood. I'd never been there, but Sam led the way like she had a GPS in her head.

As we got closer we started seeing people again: kids and grown-ups going through their Saturday-morning routines. It was super weird that none of them knew less than a mile away a mob of slimebies was trying to take over the world.

I had a sudden urge to run up to a guy mowing his lawn and tell him everything, but I knew it wouldn't do any good. No grown-up was going to believe what Sam and I had to say. No grown-up except Professor Quandary. And I still wasn't sure we could even trust *him*.

The Conference Center turned out to be a lumpy, modern

building with a banner hanging over the entrance: WELCOME TO THE AMERICA'S GOT SCIENCE JUNIOR REGIONAL TRYOUTS. There were a bunch of science symbols on one end of the banner and a big photo of Professor Quandary smiling on the other.

"Nine thirty exactly," Sam said, checking her watch for the five-hundredth time. She scanned the street, peering up and down for cars.

I heard tires behind us and turned around. An SUV and camera van from the local news channel were pulling into the Conference Center's side driveway. A bunch of people climbed out, unpacked expensive-looking equipment from the van, and began carrying it into the building. My insides went all watery. If we managed to fix everything in time, Sam and I would wind up standing right in front of those cameras, trying to win the tryouts.

Honestly, right then, I wasn't sure if that or the slimebies scared me more.

"It's him! It's him!"

I jumped. Sam had shouted the words almost right in my ear. I turned back around to find her pointing dramatically at a yellow cab coming down the road.

"How do I look?" Sam said, spinning to face me. "Do I look like the greatest young scientist of our generation?"

"How would I know?" I said. "You look nice. And your lab coat is very, you know . . . clean."

"Thank you!" Sam was bouncing up and down on her toes. The taxi came nearer and nearer. I could just make out someone in the back seat with a whole lot of shiny white hair.

Sam was almost hyperventilating as the car came to a stop right in front of us.

"I say, a welcome party!" said a voice, and Professor Quandary got out of the cab. The driver got out, too, heaving two suitcases out of the trunk before driving away.

Professor Quandary sounded just as warm and enthusiastic as he did on his TV show, but up close I noticed he had bags under his eyes. Maybe he didn't get a good night's sleep, either.

"I'm always happy to meet fans," he went on, smiling, "but I was told the mayor would be meeting me here. And unless one of you is the youngest mayor in history—"

"We're not the mayor!" cut in Sam. She was still bouncing up and down. "I'm Sam Baptiste, and this is Billy Hamilton. We're scientists like you, and we're competing in the tryouts, and—"

But it was Professor Quandary's turn to cut her off. "Ah, ah-ah," he said, raising a hand. "Then I'm afraid I can't give you any more time. It wouldn't be fair to the other contestants."

"You don't understand," I said. "We really need—"

"Oh, I suppose an autograph wouldn't do any harm," he said. "But it'll have to be quick. There's so much to do before the tryouts start. Look, see? The TV crew has just arrived."

He pointed over at the TV news van. I looked, and blinked, and frowned.

Half the expensive-looking gear was still sitting on the ground beside the van. The doors of the SUV were still open. But there was no sign of the crew. Why were they leaving their stuff out like that? Why hadn't they come back out of the building?

Sam didn't have time for news crews. She pulled out a piece of paper and a pen, and practically threw them at Professor Quandary.

"I'm a big, BIG fan," she said as he signed the paper. It was like she'd forgotten all about the *LIAR* my grandma had written across his picture. "But yeah, okay, we have to talk to you because our experiment went wrong, and you're the only one who can help, and—"

"Kids, kids! I already told you. I can't provide any help, advice, or hints that might give you an advantage in the contest. Scientists should always play fair."

"But this is a major problem!" Sam said, louder. "We made this slime, and it went bad, and now—"

Professor Quandary put his hands over his ears. "I cannot hear you," he said. "I am an objective scientist, and nothing will impact my decision this afternoon."

He kept talking as he turned and picked up his bags. Sam kept talking, too, even though Professor Quandary was already walking away, marching up the brick path to the Conference Center's front doors. If we were going to get through to him, it looked like it was up to me.

"I'M MARIANA HAMILTON'S GRANDSON!" I shouted so loud it echoed off the building.

Professor Quandary stopped dead.

"What did you say?" he said without turning around.

"Mariana Hamilton was my grandma," I said. Why was my voice shaky? "And we found a photo, so we know you two worked together. We also found her lab book, and—"

Professor Quandary whirled around.

"You found her lab book?" he demanded. "Where is it? Do you have it here?"

Sam looked at me, her eyes as wide and surprised as mine.

"N-no," she said. "No, we don't."

Professor Quandary's face was whiter than usual. "Well, please tell me you didn't try any of the experiments in there. No one knows as well as I do how dangerous Mariana's scientific inquiries were, and—"

This time he interrupted himself. He stopped with his mouth hanging open and looked back and forth between us.

"Slime," he said. "One of you said something about slime. Did one of you mention slime?"

Sam nodded. "I did. See, we ran out of time and were looking for—"

"Please, please tell me you didn't try one of *her* slime experiments."

"That's what we've been trying to tell you!" Sam sounded more annoyed than impressed with her hero now. "We made a batch of the WORLD'S MOST POWERFUL SLIME, and it's sort of, well . . ."

She trailed off, but Professor Quandary finished for her.

"Sort of making all the grown-ups into zombies. Sort of making them make more slime." He dropped his bags and sank dramatically onto his knees on the bricks. His floppy hair looked like it was deflating. "Sort of trying to take over the world."

"Um, yeah," I said. Professor Quandary was staring in horror at the ground. "So, what should we do?"

"It's happening again," whispered Professor Quandary. "Again."

"Professor!" Sam snapped her fingers. "How do we stop this? You're the only person we know who believes us, and the slime has already infected dozens of—"

"Dozens, you say?" Professor Quandary looked up. His eyes darted back and forth between us. "It's spread that far?"

We both nodded. Professor Quandary looked terrified.

"That means you must have done the experiment absolutely perfectly, kids," he said.

Sam actually looked pleased with herself.

Professor Quandary's eyes came back into focus. "Okay, one piece of good news is that a standard batch is only enough slime to take over about sixty adults, and it sounds like it's close to hitting that point. Fortunately, there *is* an antidote, but you must act quickly while there's time left to fix this. You said you still have Mariana's notes? Her lab book?"

We glanced at each other. Technically the slimebies had it, but Professor Quandary didn't wait for an answer.

"Well, in there, you'll find instructions for making the WORLD'S WORST SLIME."

"I saw that one when we were looking for a project!" said Sam.

"That's your antidote," Professor Quandary said. "Make a batch of that—make it *perfectly*—and feed it to the slime zombies—"

"We call them slimebies," I interrupted.

"Slimebies, fine! Feed that to each and every slimebie, and they'll go back to normal. But you have to make sure you get them all." He pointed at me. "Where are the slimebies now?"

"Mostly at my house," I said.

"Then let's cross our fingers they stay there," said Professor Quandary. "They do tend to stay together unless they're out hunting down more slime components, which is their one driving need. But the slime also *learns* from every person it takes over, you see. And since it's one slime operating dozens of bodies, what one of them knows, they all know. You've got to make that antidote before it spreads!" His eyes darted around nervously. The morning wasn't super warm, but Professor Quandary was sweating.

"We will!" said Sam. "You can count on us!"

"I hope so, kids. But listen, there's one more vital piece of information we need—one key ingredient—and it matters for the antidote as well. Once the WORLD'S MOST

POWERFUL SLIME was made, did it look glowing and golden at first . . . before changing colors?"

"Yeah!" I said. "We were wondering about that."

"The golden glow is what it looks like before it's *activated*. The color changing happens after. So, what we desperately need to know is which of you was the first to t—"

"Oh, hello!"

The voice came from behind Professor Quandary, and we all jumped. An older white lady was coming toward us down the brick path. The Conference Center doors stood open behind her.

For a moment her broad smile and her greeting made me instantly suspicious, but then I remembered those were actually normal ways to greet someone. I was just getting paranoid.

"Ah, Madame Mayor, I presume," said Professor Quandary in his TV voice. He got to his feet and held out a hand. "These local children were just welcoming me to your beautiful town!"

I looked over at Sam and saw she was frowning. She must have been wondering the same thing I was. Right when Professor Quandary had been about to reveal the key secret ingredient, the mayor had to come along and distract him. The mayor who was still smiling broadly, and whose loose ponytail was conveniently covering her ears . . .

Sam caught my eye and mouthed "*Slimebie?*" I shrugged one shoulder and glanced over to check on the TV news van. The crew was still nowhere to be seen.

"I want to thank you for meeting me like this," Professor Quandary said as the mayor reached us. He took her hand. "I imagine you must have plenty of work to do getting things ready!"

"We have work to do," said the mayor.

"Um, yes," said Professor Quandary.

"Work, work, work!" And in one quick move the mayor yanked Professor Quandary into a hug.

"No!" Sam yelled. "Stop!" But it was too late. A glistening, gleaming glob of silver-blue slime appeared from under the mayor's hair and smooshed its way onto Professor Quandary's cheek.

"More, more, more," the mayor said, holding Professor Quandary tight.

Professor Quandary yelled, trying to push her away. Then all at once he stopped, shuddered, and went still.

The mayor released him.

Professor Quandary straightened up.

"Oh, hello, honeys," he said, an unnaturally wide smile

spreading across his face, showing every one of his perfect teeth. A trail of slime glistened on his cheek, leading directly into his ear.

Professor Quandary—our very last hope for fixing things—had become a slimebie.

CHAPTER SEVENTEEN

(Sam)

"We gotta get out of here," Billy hissed, tugging at my arm with his entire body. But I was frozen, locked in place. I'd never seen someone get slimebied, and maybe it was weird, but I was fascinated.

Slimebie Professor Quandary smiled at us, swaying slightly just like the mayor, but I thought I maybe saw an extra sparkle in his eye. Was that the slime taking over? Or was Professor Quandary fighting back?

"Sam, come *on*!"

I finally gave in, backing away with Billy until, with the slimebies watching, we took off running the way we came. We didn't stop until we'd reached our own neighborhood.

"Okay, this is really bad," Billy said as we slowed to a walk. "The slime has spread way more than we thought.

First the mayor, then Professor Quandary—and did you see that news crew go inside and never come back out? The Conference Center must be *full* of slimebies by now."

"Hey, easy," I said. For some reason I was feeling sort of giddy. "Didn't Professor Quandary say something about the slime only being able to control up to sixty people at once? At least we know it can't get much worse." I tilted my head to one side. "I wonder *why* it can only take over sixty people. It must have to do with how much slime has to stay in each brain in order to slimebify someone."

"I guess," Billy said.

"We should do the math! This could be useful scientific data! Okay, so the batch we made filled a five hundred milliliter beaker. Take that and divide it by sixty brains, and that means each brain has a bit over eight milliliters of slime floating around in it, on average."

"Sam . . ."

"But wait, not at the beginning! Your mom must have had *all* the slime in her brain, and then most of it squelched over to your dad. It must leave just enough behind to control the person plus some extra to make more slimebies. And the rest moves on."

"Sam . . ."

"Isn't it interesting that earwax doesn't seem to change

the slime's chemical composition? It must get covered in it chugging in and out of people's ears all day. Ooh, maybe once the slime's activated it becomes chemically stable. Hey, what *is* earwax anyway?"

"SAM!"

I looked over at Billy walking beside me. His face was pink again.

"Can we maybe *not* talk about my parents having slime for brains right now?" he said.

I held up my hands. "Right. Sorry. I got carried away. We *should* be planning how we're going to get past the slimebies so we can steal the lab book back from your bathroom and make the antidote."

"Yes!" Billy nodded as we turned the corner onto the next street. "And that's not gonna be easy. How are we even— Quick! Get down!"

I didn't need telling twice. I'd seen them, too.

What looked like the entire horde of slimebies was coming down the road, directly toward us.

Billy and I dove behind a big plastic garbage can, peering around the sides to see.

The slimebies were moving in a tight formation in the very middle of the street, keeping up a steady, stamping jog. Billy's mom and dad were right in front. The sound of their feet echoed off the houses. Their unending smiles stretched across their faces.

Weirdly, several of the slimebies were carrying large plastic buckets. And from the way they were hunched over, whatever was inside must've been heavy.

We stayed hidden as the pack stomped past, turned the corner, and continued out of sight.

I looked at Billy. Billy looked at me. We both knew where the slimebies must be heading.

"Whoa," said Billy as we got to our feet. "What do you think would have happened if they'd seen us?"

I shook my head. The slimebies hadn't directly threatened Billy and me before, but they also hadn't gone running through the neighborhood like a pack of wolves on the hunt. That many smiling grown-ups, all moving and thinking as one, was bone-chilling. My giddy mood was completely gone.

"What I want to know," I said, "is what was in those buckets."

"I have a theory about that," said Billy. "But we have to get back to my place to be sure."

He did not sound excited at the thought.

When we reached Billy's house, we found the front door hanging open, creaking ominously in the breeze. We edged inside . . . and straight into a scene from a horror movie.

The walls, ceilings, and floors of the entire downstairs were covered in toxic-green spinach stains. Dirty bowls, pots, and mugs littered every surface. The tables and chairs were all shoved around, blocking doorways and crammed into the corners. Books had been knocked off shelves, picture frames hung crooked on the walls, and there were dirty, sticky shoe prints all over the floors. It was as different from the pristine house I'd seen only a day ago as it could have possibly been.

"Wow," said Billy, blowing out his cheeks and wiping a smear of spinach soup from a light switch. "I thought it looked bad in here last night! It looks so much worse all empty like this. But at least they're gone."

"Come on, come on," I said, tugging him toward the bathroom. "We have to see if the slimebies took the lab book with them. If they did, we can pretty much say goodbye to the world!"

The door to the downstairs bathroom wasn't just open, it was hanging off its hinges, and waiting inside was the biggest mess of all. Our beautiful scientific equipment was scattered across the floor; empty bottles of glue and shaving cream filled the sink; chains of toilet paper hung from the shower rod and the back of the toilet; and the tub, stained with ring after ring of golden, rainbow-sheened slime, was empty.

Billy's neat and tidy parents would have started steaming from the ears if they could have seen it. And if their ears weren't full of slime.

"I was right!" Billy said, pointing at the tub. "Those buckets must have been full of the new slime! They took it all with them."

"Thank the entire universe they didn't take this, though!" I pulled Mariana Hamilton's lab book from the back of the sink where it was propped behind the hot and cold taps. "What I really don't get," I said, hugging it, "is why they would all suddenly decide to go running off to the Conference Center. It doesn't make sense."

Billy looked very serious. "I have a guess. I think maybe it has to do with what Professor Quandary said about the slime learning from each person it takes over."

"Huh? Explain, please."

"Well, Professor Quandary knows the secret missing ingredient or whatever, right? That means the slime learned it, too, the second it squidged inside his ear and got to his brain. So, all the slimebies know it now. Remember how they were chanting *Find what's missing*? Of course they all went running to him."

I snapped my fingers. "That's right! Okay, but wait, why

move the slime? Why go to all that trouble? Why bring the slime to him instead of bringing Professor Quandary back here?"

Billy shrugged. "I don't know. I never said it *all* made sense." He thought. "Maybe slimebie Professor Quandary thinks the secret ingredient is somewhere at the Conference Center? Or might be arriving there soon?"

We looked at each other. Kids and parents from all over the region were on their way to the Conference Center right now. That was ominous. We both shivered.

"Let's take this one step at a time," I said, using one of my mom's favorite phrases. Dang, I really hoped she was still safe at home. She wouldn't like being a slimebie one bit. "We've got the house to ourselves, your grandma's equipment back, and your grandma's book, so let's get working. You get the sink cleared and start rinsing out beakers, and I'll look over the new experiment."

I'd only glanced at the page for the WORLD'S WORST SLIME before, so it was a huge relief to find out it wasn't nearly as complicated as the WORLD'S MOST POWERFUL SLIME.

"Equal parts glue, shaving cream, and white vinegar to start," I read out loud. "Wait, motor oil?" I groaned. "Where are we supposed to get that?"

"That's no problem," said Billy, scrubbing at the sink. "I can drain some oil from my mom's motorcycle."

"You know how to do that?" I was impressed.

"She makes me help her when she does oil changes. She says it'll be useful for when I'm older."

"Well, it's useful now! Remind me to thank your mom."

"Keep reading the ingredients," said Billy.

"*Components*."

"Whatever."

I read the rest of the page out loud while Billy cleaned, and just like before, we split up the work, hunting down what we needed around the ruined house. Luck, or maybe Mariana Hamilton, was on our side because twenty minutes later we'd found every component on the list.

There was just one problem.

"Okay, I found a can of anchovies at the back of the pantry," Billy said. "But I only got a few tablespoons of juice out of it." He held up a small jar. "And the book is super specific about using equal portions. If we can only use this much of everything, we're not going to make a whole lot of slime."

"And we need enough to feed sixty slimebies," I said. I frowned. "Well, we'll just have to do the best we can with what's in front of us."

"Have you always talked exactly like your mom?" asked Billy.

I threw an empty glue bottle at him.

Mixing the WORLD'S WORST SLIME was going to take at least twenty minutes. The instructions weren't difficult to follow, but things needed to be added in a precise order and stirred a certain number of times, and since we'd have to use every drop of our anchovy juice, we didn't have any room for error.

I ran things, of course, with Billy as my assistant, and I couldn't help feeling proud. This was the second real-life science experiment I'd done in three days. And sure, the first one had led to some not-so-good results, but Professor Quandary—*the* Professor Quandary—had also told me right to my face that I'd done it perfectly.

I wanted the satisfaction of doing a perfect job again.

Finally, we got to the last step. Billy passed me a test tube of motor oil that he'd drained from his mom's bike and kept warm over the steam from the hot tap, and I carefully poured it into the rest of the mixture.

The reaction was like pure magic. No, it was better than magic; it was pure chemistry! The lumpy shaving foam dissolved into the vinegar, the watery anchovy juice melded with the glue, and suddenly everything came together to form two cups of swirling, gloppy goop.

Billy caught my eye over the beaker and I instantly knew what he was thinking.

"Guess we know how it gets its name now, don't we?" I said.

Because this was, without a doubt, the world's worst slime. It was oozy and blotchy and weirdly chunky. It looked like a hundred melted slugs mixed with Shredded Wheat, with an oily sheen on top. I shook the beaker, and it glopped side to side, leaving a yellow-brown film and air bubbles that filled and burst like blisters.

And as bad as it looked, it smelled even worse.

"I don't care what you say," said Billy, holding a hand over his nose. "I am *not* touching that stuff."

I shook the beaker again, breathing through my mouth to avoid the smell. "No one said you had to. What I want to know is how we're supposed to get *sixty* full-grown slime-bies to taste it."

We tossed ideas back and forth, looking for anything that might help us. I was starting to get seriously frustrated when I noticed a tiny note written in the margin of the slime experiment. It was so small I almost thought it was a smudge. I peered closer.

A little goes a long way.

That was all it said.

I looked back at the beaker of horrible slime. Then I looked out the bathroom door, suddenly thinking about the mess of pots in the kitchen.

I jumped to my feet, slamming the lab book shut and hugging it again. Billy gave a little scream.

"Don't do that!" he said. "Are you trying to scare me to death?"

"I figured it out!" I said. "I've totally got it!" And really, it was so obvious.

"Okay," said Billy. "What?"

"Spinach soup!"

Billy wrinkled his forehead. "Spinach soup?"

I opened the book, pointing to the note. "Your grandma says right here that a little of this stuff goes a long way. So, what if we add it to a big batch of that icy spinach-honey soup the slimebies love so much?"

Billy's forehead relaxed as he understood. "Then they won't be able to stop themselves from eating it, just like last night." He shuddered at the memory.

"See?" I said. "It'll work!"

"Okay, but new problem," said Billy. "I know for a fact that there is *zero* spinach left in this house. Apart from what's smeared on the walls."

"Then we'll just have to get some more," I said. "You've still got that change your mom let you keep, right?"

Billy blinked and patted his pocket. "Yeah, about sixty bucks."

"Well, I hope that'll buy us enough at the store," I said, my hands on my hips. "This spinach soup is literally the world's only hope."

CHAPTER EIGHTEEN

(Billy)

It was the strangest feeling, walking the familiar route through our silent, empty neighborhood. Apart from one slamming door and a few scared-looking kids peering out windows, we might have been the only people in the world.

Things got worse when we reached the EZ-Shop.

There were no cars out front. No one returning their cart. The sliding glass doors were still. The warm spring air felt tense and close.

Sam led the way inside. The checkout lanes were deserted. The shopping music wheezing through the overhead speakers made the emptiness feel that much more ominous.

"Hello?" yelled Sam. "Anybody?"

We waited.

There was no reply.

"Guess we have the place to ourselves," said Sam. "Come on, this way."

I followed after her, instinctively looking down every aisle we passed, ready to see slimebies stumbling toward us. But there was no one.

A green sign shaped like a piece of broccoli announced the produce department was around the next corner. I followed close behind Sam, only realizing she'd stopped dead after I'd bumped into her.

"What's wrong?" I whispered.

Sam pointed.

The wall of fresh produce had a gap in it. On one side of the gap was a display of crisp lettuce. On the other were bins of green beans. And between them, under a plastic tag that said SPINACH, there was nothing. Not one leaf. The black plastic shelves were cracked and broken, like they'd been through a battle, and the mist sprayer over them was hanging crooked.

Sam whistled. "Looks like they beat us to it."

"But . . . that can't be *all* of it," I said, glancing around. "There has to be more spinach around here somewhere. Maybe in one of those pre-bagged salads?"

We looked, but every scrap of spinach in the entire produce department was gone. Sam and I locked eyes over a stack of red peppers. "Should we check in the back?" she asked. "We're probably really, super not allowed in there. But this is kind of an emergency."

"What about the deli? Maybe they kept a supply for putting on sandwiches?"

"Good thinking. You check there; I'll check the back."

Sam disappeared through a set of swinging doors in the corner by the milk, and I headed for the deli. I was all alone now.

At least, I hoped I was. I winced every time my shoes squeaked on the shiny floor, and by the time I reached the deli I had the skin-crawling feeling that I was definitely being watched.

The deli counter seemed to go on and on, but I finally found a door at the far end that said STAFF ONLY. I braced myself and slipped through.

It was so weird being on the other side of the counter. There were metal rolling racks of food, stacks of cardboard boxes, rows of silver drawers on wheels, knives hanging from the wall, slicing machines, and clear plastic tubs of chopped vegetables, sliced meat, and pickles everywhere, along with about a thousand jumbo-sized buckets of mayonnaise.

And still not a single grown-up in sight.

I shivered. Was everyone who worked here a slimebie

now? It sure looked that way. Or maybe some of them saw what was happening to their friends and ran home to hide.

I couldn't blame them.

I poked around, opening cupboards and mini fridges and drawers, but didn't find any sign of hidden spinach. I was heading back to the door, hoping Sam had had more luck, when the prickly feeling of being watched rolled over me again. Much, much stronger.

I froze. My eyes scanned the deli.

"Hello?" I said. My voice came out all high and raspy. I almost sounded like a slimebie. "Is someone there?"

Nothing.

I took two careful steps forward. The STAFF ONLY door was about thirty feet away. If I ran as soon as I was past that pile of mayonnaise buckets . . .

My next careful step caught the edge of one of the rolling tray stands, making it rattle.

"GET AWAY! GET AWAY! THERE'S NO MORE LEFT!"

The mayonnaise buckets went flying as somebody jumped out from underneath them, waving a loaf of French bread like a sword.

"YOU CAN'T SCARE ME!" the stranger yelled, sounding scared out of his wits.

I suddenly realized I was flat against the deli counter, holding a bag of salt-and-vinegar chips in front of me like a shield, my heart hammering hard enough to break my ribs.

The stranger and I looked at each other. Only, wait, it wasn't a stranger. It was the tall teenager with long black hair and a lip ring. The deli clerk who'd given us our first jar of pickle juice.

The last time we met, Sam had said he reminded her of a zombie. She wouldn't have said that now. Bored-teenage-deli-clerk looked wide awake and terrified.

"Oh," he said, eyeing me and my bag of chips. "It's only you. Pickle-juice kid. Thank goodness. I thought maybe . . . *they* were back." He shuddered. I actually heard the buckets at his feet rattle.

"You thought *who* were back?" I asked, although he had to mean the slimebies. Did this mean teenagers were safe from becoming slimebies, too? Or was he just really good at hiding?

"Haven't you seen them?" the boy said. "The adults! First they want all our pickles, and that's weird but okay, what-ever. Then they buy up all the spinach. And I mean ALL the spinach. And *then*, then they clean out the entire supply of honey. And buckets! And every time there are more of them! And they're always smiling! Why, pickle-juice kid?" He shook his loaf of bread at me. "*Why are they always smiling?*"

"Okay, okay," I said, holding out my chips and setting them carefully on the nearest table. "We're gonna be okay." It felt so weird to be reassuring a high schooler. "I'm Billy," I said. "Billy Hamilton."

"I'm Zack." The boy exhaled hard. "Zack Grocer."

"Wait, really?"

"Yes. Zack *Grocer*. And yes, I work at a *grocery* store, and I promise I've heard every single joke already, so can we please drop it?"

I dropped it, forcing down my smile.

"So, why are you back here, kid?" Zack asked. He'd lowered his loaf of bread, apparently deciding he was safe around me.

"It's Billy. And my friend and I are here because, um, well, we need spinach, too. Lots and *lots* of spinach."

Zack started to laugh.

"We know there's no more in the produce section," I said, talking over him. "But we thought maybe there would be some here for sandwiches or something?"

"Well, there's not!" Zack's laughter was a little scary. And he was shouting. "They got it all! Every last bit! You and your friend are out of luck!"

"WANNA BET?"

This shout came from across the store. Zack and I both ducked behind the counter, then raised our heads to peer out through the deli case.

Sam was holding open the doors that led to the back, grinning triumphantly. I stood all the way up, and Zack cautiously joined me.

"You find a new friend, Billy?" Sam yelled. "Well, I found something even better! You two quit playing around and get back here. It's time for some teamwork. Recess is over!"

She disappeared, leaving the doors swinging.

Zack looked over at me. I looked at Zack.

"Why does your friend sound like my old elementary school principal?" he said.

Before I could answer, Sam's voice rang out again from between the doors.

"And bring me a shopping cart!"

CHAPTER NINETEEN

(Sam)

The doors leading to the back room flew open with a bang.

"Over here!" I called, waving as Billy pushed the cart through. He headed over, staring around at the tall shelves covered in pallets of cans and boxes. I'd done the same thing. Behind the scenes at the grocery store was kind of depressing: all cardboard and concrete and gloomy fluorescent lights. Nothing like the bright, glossy store out front. To be totally honest, I was glad to have company.

A teenager stepped through the doors behind Billy.

"Hey," he said. "I'm Zack."

"Sam." I recognized him by his lip ring: the zombie kid from the deli counter. So, it looked like the slime wasn't interested in taking over teenagers? Interesting. More useful data.

"So, what'd you want the cart for?" Billy asked.

"Yeah." Zack scuffed one of his boots against the concrete. "And this kid says you're looking for spinach? I promise you there's no spinach back here. The grown-ups already cleaned out the walk-in refrigerator."

"My name is Billy," said Billy. Zack ignored him.

"There's no *fresh* spinach," I said, shooting Zack a look. "But if you think a little harder, and you know where to look . . ."

I led them over to a big silver door set into a wall and tugged on the two-foot handle. The door opened, letting out a freezing blast of air. The two boys followed me inside, where more shelves lining the walls were stacked with cardboard boxes, including an open one packed to the brim with packages of . . .

"*Frozen* spinach!" I yelled over the whirring freezer fans, my arms raised in victory.

"Genius!" Billy yelled back.

"I'm freezing!" hollered Zack.

We got to work, and within a couple minutes our cart was piled to the top with dozens of plastic-wrapped frozen spinach blocks.

"Ahh, much better," I said as I wheeled our prize back into the main store, which suddenly felt like a tropical paradise.

The music was still burbling along to itself. The place was still deserted.

Billy and Zack had their hands tucked under their armpits to warm them up.

"Okay, so who's the greatest young scientist of her generation?" I said, turning to them.

"You are," said Billy. "I never would have thought of checking the freezer section. And it looks like the slimebies didn't, either."

Zack was looking back and forth between me and Billy. "Did this kid just use the word *slimebies*?" he asked.

I nodded. "He did. And his name's Billy. Slimebies are what we call all those grown-ups you were hiding from."

"Under your mayonnaise buckets," Billy added with a grin.

"Got it, sure." Zack was nodding. "And you need spinach like they did because . . . ?"

"We made an antidote slime," I explained. "An anti-*slimy*-dote, and we're going to get them to eat it by mixing it into cold spinach soup. Slimebies *love* cold spinach soup."

"Gross," said Zack. "But okay, what's up with the honey? Why did they buy all of that, too?"

I smacked myself on the forehead. "Honey! I almost forgot! Zack, you stay here and guard the cart. Billy, come with me!"

"Aisle seven," Zack called after us as we sprinted away.

"Please, please, please let there be some left," I whispered, turning at a shampoo display to run down aisle seven.

There was a ragged gap in the shelves here, too, but luck was on our side again. It took Billy getting right down on his stomach on the floor, but he finally spotted one last jumbo jar of honey hiding way back in the darkness on the bottom shelf.

"Whew!" he said, dusting himself off. "I hope this is enough."

"It'll have to be," I said. We rejoined Zack, and I added the honey to the spinach cart, wheeling the whole thing to the front of the store. It was super heavy.

"Um, what are you doing?" asked Zack as I pushed the cart into a checkout lane.

"Paying, of course." I looked to Billy. He nodded.

"Oh." Zack looked super surprised. "Those, uh, slimebie people didn't."

"Well, we're not slimebies," Billy said. "We're scientists. I mean, Sam definitely is, at least."

I smiled at him.

"Who's gonna take your money, though?" Zack sure did like asking questions.

"You are," I said.

Zack looked from us to the overflowing cart to the register. He groaned.

"Fii-iiine."

He walked around to the register.

"Hello and welcome to EZ-Shop. Did you find everything you were looking for today?" he droned, sounding like a computer.

Billy and I laughed.

"Yes, thank you."

"Did you bring your own bags?" droned Zack.

I looked at Billy. "I think we're just going to use the cart?" he answered. "If that's okay?"

Zack shrugged and tapped at the cash register screen. "Set your items on the belt, please."

It took a long time to scan all the bricks of frozen spinach. Billy fetched an empty cart to throw them in instead of bagging, and for several long minutes there was only the *thunk* as I set the frozen spinach on the conveyor belt, the beep of Zack's scanner, and the clang as Billy tossed them in the cart.

"Hey, these are starting to get slippery," Billy said as we neared the end. "They're already thawing out."

I nodded. "That's okay. We want them to soften a bit so we can make them into soup. So long as they're still cold, we should be fine."

Finally, all the spinach and the jar of honey had been scanned and moved from one cart to the other.

"That'll be fifty-nine dollars and ninety-five cents," droned Zack, reading off the register screen. "Will that be cash or card?"

"Cash," said Billy, handing over his money. We shared a look. There was just barely enough. We sure were running through our fair share of good luck today.

Zack handed Billy his receipt and a nickel.

"Thank you for shopping at EZ-Shop. Have a pleasant day."

"Thanks for all your help!" I said.

Billy started pulling the cart around, aiming for the doors. I looked over at Zack. He was sitting on the checker stool, looking bored and maybe a little sad.

"What are you going to do?" I asked.

Zack shrugged. "Stay here to keep an eye on the store, I guess. And wait to see if you two manage to fix all those slimebies. I mean, you'll come back and let me know, right?"

His voice got really sad then, and I suddenly realized: Zack, the too-cool-for-you high school guy, was jealous of our mission.

"Tell you what," I said. "Why don't you let the store take care of itself and come with us?"

Zack and Billy both looked at me.

"Really?" said Billy.

"Really?" said Zack.

"Yup." I nodded. "This way you'll know right away when the slimebies have been conquered."

"Or when they've taken over the world," Billy said. "Either way."

"Sweet!" For three whole seconds Zack's face totally changed, gleaming with excitement like a kindergartner with a cookie. Then he snapped back to being a moody teenager. "I mean, you know, sure," he said. "Whatever."

I clapped my hands the way my mom did before announcing chores. "Great! Then you get to be in charge of pushing the cart."

CHAPTER TWENTY

(Still Sam)

We trooped out of the EZ-Shop back into the sunny afternoon, Billy and me leading the way, Zack and the cart following behind.

It was such a relief to be outside that it took me several blocks to realize we were taking the same route Billy and I had the day before. That meant we'd be passing Mrs. Hubble's house. Billy seemed to be thinking the same thing I was, and as the house came into view we both slowed down until, without speaking, we came to a stop outside her fence.

"Whoa," Billy said, staring at the garden.

"Totally," said Zack.

I already knew Mrs. Hubble had pulled up all her prized sunflowers—she'd gotten enough dirt from them on Billy's floor—but I still wasn't prepared for what that had done to her yard. The house and most of the garden still looked like something out of a fairy tale, butterflies and all, but right along the fence was a long jagged scar, an ugly open gash of rocks and crumbling dirt.

"She is going to be *so* angry once she's un-slimebified," Billy said, shaking his head. "And confused, probably. But I bet mostly angry."

"Maybe she'll decide her dog was just digging or something?" I said. I looked around the yard. "Hey, where is her dog anyway?"

The wheels of the shopping cart squeaked as the three of us inched the tiniest bit closer to the fence. Billy stood on his tiptoes and leaned forward, craning his neck just enough to see over the PRIVATE PROPERTY signs . . .

. . . and Gilbert the guard dog erupted from underneath a lilac bush, barking and slobbering and showing all of his ten thousand teeth.

"Aahhh!" Billy and I yelled together, leaping at least five feet back in one go.

Thank goodness slimebie Mrs. Hubble hadn't ripped her fence out along with her sunflowers! Thank goodness she hadn't let her killer dog out onto the streets! Thank goodness the slime had somehow remembered to close the . . . oh . . . no.

"Billy!" I screamed, pointing, and Billy looked, but it was

too late. Gilbert had spotted the half-open gate, too, and before we could even blink, he was out of the yard and scrabbling across the concrete toward us.

Billy and I scampered up the side of the shopping cart so fast you would've thought it was a jungle gym.

I tried to shout out a warning for Zack, but before I could make a sound he *knelt down* on the sidewalk and opened both arms wide!

I almost couldn't look. Gilbert was barking nonstop. His tongue was hanging out of his mouth. His eyes were rolling.

"Boosh-boosh!" cried Zack as the wild dog leapt straight for his face . . .

. . . and started licking his ears.

Wait. What?

What was happening?

"Boosh-buh-boosh. Oh, yes you are! Shoo-buh-shoo!" Zack said, his face only inches from the dog's. "Who wants his neck scratched? Uh-shoo-buh-doo? Uh-shoo-buh-doo!"

Billy and I gaped from our spot on top of the slimy half-frozen spinach.

"Umm, Zack?" My voice was kind of croaky. "What are you doing?"

Zack looked up. "Dog talk. I'm just saying hey to my buddy here."

"You know Gilbert?" Billy sounded as freaked out as I was.

"Of course," Zack said. "I take him on walks when Mrs. Hubble goes on her skiing trips to Italy."

"Mrs. Hubble goes on skiing trips to Italy?!"

"Sheesh, calm down, you two," said Zack. "Anyway, aren't we supposed to be in a hurry or something?"

I looked over at Billy. "He's right. We need to get this spinach out of the sun. We won't have time to re-chill it if it melts too much. And since I guess we're safe . . . ?"

Slowly, carefully, Billy and I climbed down from the cart. Gilbert gave us a few enthusiastic sniffs, then went back to having his neck scratched. It looked like he'd decided any friends of Zack's were friends of his.

The empty neighborhood didn't feel quite so eerie the rest of the way back. The mission had been a success. We had a shopping cart full of spinach, the very last jar of honey, and—definitely a surprise but maybe best of all—two unexpected new friends.

CHAPTER TWENTY-ONE

(Billy)

Back at my house we wasted no time and wheeled that shopping cart right through the front door and into the kitchen, leaving Gilbert out front to keep watch in case the slimebie army decided to come back.

"Duuuude," Zack said, staring around at the green handprints all over the walls and the spinach-stained dishes scattered everywhere. "You live here?"

I nodded. "It's not like this all the time, though. This is just from the surprise slimebie slumber party last night."

"Slimebies," he repeated. He shook his head. "I really don't get this slime-zombie thing. What do they even *want*?"

"Professor Quandary says slimebies mostly just want components to make more slime," said Sam. "So that they can turn *more* grown-ups into slimebies."

"And then those slimebies will take over even more grown-ups," I added. "I guess until there aren't any normal grown-ups left."

Zack whistled. "So, you two might have set off the end of the world as we know it?"

"Yes, but *accidentally*," said Sam. "And now we're going to save it."

She marched over to the downstairs bathroom and came back with the beaker of the WORLD'S WORST SLIME.

"Pee-yew!" said Zack, holding his nose. "What is that stuff?"

"That's the antidote," I said. It really did smell, even through the plastic wrap I'd used to cover the top. "It's going in the cold spinach-honey soup. Once we make it."

Sam gave a determined nod, but Zack frowned.

"How are you planning to get the slimebies to eat it, though?" he asked. "Are you going to make, like, a bowl for each of them, mix in a drop of that, and just hand them out?"

It was my turn to frown. "That's a good point." I turned to Sam. "How *are* we going to get them to eat their own share? Last night they were practically fighting over the big soup pot. If we hand out single servings they'll mob whichever slimebie has one and it'll just get spilled."

"We'll have to somehow serve one big batch they can all get to," said Sam. "Any ideas?"

We stared around my wrecked home. The empty soup pot lying on the dining table was the biggest container I could think of. Well, except for the bathtub where the slimebies made their new slime. The bathtub would actually be perfect, if we had any way of taking it with us. Wait . . .

"Maybe we could, like, line the shopping cart with plastic bags or something?" Zack said with a shrug.

I saw Sam's eyes going as wide as mine.

"The kiddie pool!" we shouted together.

"The what?" said Zack. But Sam and I were already racing upstairs to the attic.

It was a struggle getting the hard plastic pool down the stairs, but with Zack pulling from below we managed it. I was all ready to start tearing open the frozen spinach blocks and tossing them in right there, but Sam stopped me.

"Wait wait wait!" she said. "If we make the soup in here, we'll never get it out the door!"

"You know, you're pretty smart for a fourth grader," said Zack as we rolled the kiddie pool out onto the driveway.

"And you're pretty okay for a teenager," replied Sam. "Here, let's set the pool on top of the shopping cart so we can wheel it around after."

We dumped the spinach bricks into a pile next to the cart and started unwrapping them as quickly as possible. The midday sun was beating down on us, but it wasn't long before I could feel my fingers start to go numb.

"These are so perfect!" said Sam, tossing another squishy, half-frozen green lump into the pool. "The outsides are all melted and slimy, but the insides are still ice. That's exactly what we want."

Gilbert, who'd been prowling around watching us, raised his nose to the kiddie pool, sniffed curiously, and backed away, his tail tucked between his legs.

"Well, at least we know for sure *he's* not a slimebie!" I said. "He still makes me kind of nervous, though."

"Aw, he's a big ol' softy," said Zack. He made a kissy face at Gilbert. "Aren't you, boosh-boosh? Ishn't shoo a big ol' shofty?"

Gilbert wagged his tail and stared up at Zack adoringly.

Sam and I coughed to cover our laughs.

Before long we had emptied all the spinach into the kiddie pool and cleared away the plastic packaging.

"What's next?" asked Zack.

"The honey," said Sam. "And then I guess we should start adding water, too."

Water was easy, thanks to the garden hose, and as the

pool filled, Sam turned the honey jar upside down, letting the thick golden syrup drizzle all over the spinach. The half-frozen blocks were floating now, with thawed leaves flailing out like tentacles searching for prey. The honey oozed over everything, sinking to the bottom of the cold water and gluing the slimy greens together.

When the pool was full and the jar of honey emptied, we all gathered in for the final crucial step.

Sam pulled the plastic wrap off the beaker of the WORLD'S WORST SLIME and carefully poured the slippery contents into the center of the pool. For one awful moment it looked like it was just going to congeal in a lump, but then it slowly dissolved into the gloopy mess. A few seconds later an oily brown sheen spread across the surface of our horrible creation.

"That," said Zack, "looks absolutely disgusting."

"Putrid," Sam agreed.

"Revolting," I finished.

Sam gave me a high five, but we all stepped back as the smell of the WORLD'S WORST SLIME rolled across the lawn, stronger than ever. Even the cartoon turtles on the inside of the pool looked like they were trying to escape.

"The soup must be making it even more potent," Sam said. I had my shirt pulled up over my nose. Gilbert was cowering behind a shrub with his head under his paws.

"There is no way I'm helping push that thing all the way to the Conference Center," said Zack. "It smells worse than the deli dumpsters at the end of the week!"

Sam waved at me, her nose pinched shut. "Do you have any clothespins? Or safety masks we can breathe through?"

I shook my head. "No. I mean, I can go look, but—" Then an idea hit me. "Hey, I might have something that could work. Hang on!"

I raced back into the house, taking the stairs to the attic two at a time. I quickly found what I was looking for and ran back out to the lawn.

"Voilà!" I said, presenting them with my brilliant idea.

They both stared at me.

"Novelty nose-and-mustache glasses?" Zack said. "Are you serious?"

"What?" I looked from him to Sam. "They're the reject ones my dad stashed in the attic. Remember? Because the mustaches were blocking the nose holes—I mean nostrils? If I'm right, they should act like a filter! Look."

I put on a pair with a scratchy, thick black mustache and a hot-pink nose, and marched over to the cart. I took a deep breath in and out. Only a little air got in around the sides, and I couldn't smell anything apart from the plastic nose. "See?" I said, holding my arms out and smiling.

"Billy Hamilton," said Sam, "you look absolutely ridiculous."

But she came over and took a pair of glasses from me—hers had the same black frames and mustache but a fluorescent green nose—and put them on.

"Huh!" she said, turning to Zack. "He's right, they totally work." Her voice sounded funny around the mustache.

Zack took his purple-nosed glasses from me and put them on.

"I hope you know that if photos of me looking like this ever get out, I'll have to move to Alaska," he said.

"I'm pretty sure we'll be too busy dealing with the slime-bies to stop for photos," said Sam.

We all stopped smiling at that, and something like a chill swept over us, despite the sun still beating down overhead. We were about to head *back* to the Conference Center. Deliberately. We were about to face off against an entire army of grown-ups being controlled by an evil slime. And we were doing it armed with nothing more than novelty mustache glasses and a kiddie pool full of soup.

Sam adjusted her lab coat. Zack tucked his hair behind his ears. Gilbert crept over to us from the shrub, looking unhappy but clearly planning on following wherever we led.

I nodded once. We were a long, long way from where we'd been the day Sam confronted me on the sidewalk. I felt like a completely different person. A person who finished things.

"Come on, team," I said. "Let's do this."

CHAPTER TWENTY-TWO

(Sam)

The neighborhood streets were completely silent as we made our way toward the Conference Center. Zack pushed the cart, since he was strongest, and Billy and I walked on either side, one hand on the kiddie pool to keep it steady.

I was terrified every moment we might hit a crack in the asphalt and spill it all. We were so close, and there was no chance we'd be able to make more of the antidote, or even the soup. Not before the slimebies took over the world, anyway.

Suddenly, Gilbert gave a warning bark, and Billy and I looked back. A small crowd of kids had crept out of their houses and were gathering behind us. For a second I wondered what they wanted, then I understood. First their grown-ups disappeared, and now here we came, marching down the street with our kiddie pool of slime and our mustaches. They probably guessed we knew something they didn't. And they were right.

"Hi, everyone!" I called, waving my free hand. "Stay calm. We're going to fix everything."

"Hey, Sam, do you think maybe they could help us?" Billy said.

But just then the wind shifted, and the group of kids suddenly looked like they'd fallen headfirst into a sewer. They made gagging faces, covered their mouths and noses with their hands, and quickly retreated.

The novelty nose-glasses were doing such a good job, I'd honestly forgotten about the smell coming from the kiddie pool. Looked like it was as strong as ever, though. One by one the kids disappeared, retreating to the stink-free safety of their houses.

"Oh, okay, guess not," said Billy. "Bye, kids."

"Too bad," I said. "It would have been fun to show up at the Conference Center with an army of our own."

"We would have looked like the Pied Piper of Hamelin," said Zack in his bored voice. "Only with mustaches."

"And weird-colored noses," said Billy.

"How do you know the Pied Piper didn't have a weird-colored nose?" asked Zack.

"How do you know he didn't have a mustache?"

"Can we just get to the Conference Center now, please?" I said.

We kept going, the cart wheels squeaking, on and on through the eerily silent streets.

Was this what the world was going to be like if we failed and the slime took over? Empty, lonely, and abandoned? It only took one single grown-up getting slimebied—poor Billy's mom—for all of this to start. Now we were the only ones who could stop it.

The Conference Center doors were closed again when we arrived, and there were no grown-ups in sight, slimebie or otherwise. But there were kids. Most of them looked to be about the same age as Billy and me, and all of them were dressed up in fancy *I'm-going-to-be-on-TV* outfits. Although a few super-cool kids also wore lab coats like mine.

The kids were huddled together in groups on the lawn outside the entrance, but a bunch of them came running toward us as we got nearer. I recognized a few from our grade at school, none of whom had ever spoken to me, of course, and I even spotted two from our own class: the eye-rolling girls who sat across from me at lunch. All of them started talking at once.

"What's going on?"

"Can you help us find—"

"—acting so scary—"

"—never came back out!"

"—the deal with your glasses?"

It took a while, but eventually we got everyone to calm down enough to tell us what happened. Long story short, they'd all arrived early with their parents to set up their projects for the *AMERICA'S GOT SCIENCE* tryouts, but when they got inside they were ambushed by a crowd of creepy grown-ups who then slimebified their parents.

When they saw that their parents had all suddenly started smiling and swaying and chanting about *work* and finding something that was missing, the kids had abandoned their experiments and run for their lives.

"And mine was so *good*," sobbed one boy who must've been in third grade. "It was a volcano that burped helium bubbles."

"And mine was a volcano that made edible, cinnamon-flavored lava," said a gloomy-faced girl.

"Mine was an artificial seaweed that can soak up oil spills," added a small girl I hadn't noticed yet. She looked closely at me. "Hey, aren't you Principal Baptiste's daughter?"

I nodded, wanting to ask her more about her project—it

was exactly the kind of thing Professor Quandary would love!—but to my total surprise Billy started talking.

"It's gonna be okay, everybody," he called out. All the other kids had drifted over by then, and he had the whole crowd listening. "Let us handle it. We're going inside"—several of the kids gasped—"so just wait out here and you'll be safe."

It sounded like a good, confident speech to me, but it started another four kids bawling.

"What did I say?" asked Billy.

"That's literally what the last group of parents said when they got here," one of the eye-rolling girls informed us.

Her friend pointed to the building. "And they never came back out."

I let out a long breath. "Okay, huddle time," I said to my team.

Zack, Billy, and I leaned over the kiddie pool of putrid soup. Gilbert put his paws up on the side, his head almost to my level, his ears perked. It looked like he was willing to deal with the smell if it meant being included.

"I don't think we should leave these kids on their own," I said, keeping my voice low. "They're freaking out. They need someone to look after them." Somewhere behind us another kid started crying.

"Fii-iine," Zack said. "I'll do it."

I blinked. I wasn't sure things were getting *that* bad.

"Really?" said Billy.

"Yeah," said Zack. "I'm the closest one to a grown-up around here. And didn't you two start this whole situation anyway?" We nodded. "Then, according to the ancient rules of how things work, you two have to go in there and fix it."

I didn't know what ancient rules Zack was talking about, but he had a point. He probably wouldn't be that much use inside anyway. I was about to reply when there were screams and a fresh wave of crying from the gathered kids.

"What now?" I muttered. We were trying to finalize our rescue plans here.

"Um, hey, Principal Baptiste's daughter?" came a voice. "You should probably see this."

I looked around to see artificial-seaweed girl staring at me, her eyes wide. She raised a hand and pointed back toward the building.

The doors of the Conference Center had been opened, and there, right under the banner for *AMERICA'S GOT SCIENCE*, stood a pretty woman wearing a purple silk shirt and gray pinstripe slacks. She had dark brown skin, a beautiful crown of curly black hair, and a wide, vacant, terrifying smile.

It was my mom. She was here. And she had become a slimebie.

The world around me spun. Everyone seemed to be holding their breath.

Then Gilbert barked once, twice, scaring me so much I almost knocked the kiddie pool off the shopping cart.

When I looked back, my mom had disappeared into the slimebie den of the Conference Center. Leaving the door wide open behind her.

CHAPTER TWENTY-THREE

(Billy)

For a second, I thought I was going to have to stop Sam from racing after her mom right then. I definitely couldn't blame her if she wanted to, but I needed her with me if we were gonna pull off this anti-slimey-dote plan.

Luckily Sam got extra bossy instead, and after ordering Zack and Gilbert to herd the kids around to the side of the building—hopefully out of any unexpected danger—she took over her side of the shopping cart, we gave each other a nod, and we headed in.

Moving the cart turned out to be way harder with only two people. Sam and I had to keep one hand on the pool and one on the handle, pushing and steadying and walking all at the same time. It was slow going, but the Conference Center doors loomed closer and closer.

Over our heads the banner with Professor Quandary's face flapped in the wind. The rippling vinyl made his expression shift from TV smile to slimebie smile, back and forth, over and over. It was like rewatching that last moment before he became one of them, the moment he was just about to tell us the missing secret ingredient.

I shivered. With Professor Quandary slimebified, the whole pack knew that secret ingredient now. And we still didn't.

Sam and I paused just before the doors, met each other's eyes, and charged the squeaking shopping cart inside.

The entrance hall of the Conference Center was a lot like the outside: fancy and modern. There were two big sets of stairs, plus doors and hallways leading off in multiple directions. But there were no people. Not even Sam's mom. The only thing even close was a life-sized cardboard cutout of Professor Quandary.

The grinning cutout was pointing down a hallway to our right, so we followed its lead. At the end of the hall we found another cardboard Professor Quandary, then followed its pointing finger to another. Except for our footsteps, the squealing shopping cart wheels, and the spinach sloshing around, the whole Conference Center was deadly, ominously quiet.

We went down two more long halls and around three corners, still totally alone. The kids outside said they'd left all their slimebified parents in here, so where were they now? And where were the original slimebies? And our parents? And Sam's mom and Mrs. Hubble? Were we too late to save them?

Man, I thought as we reached a final cardboard Professor Quandary announcing we were at the tryout hall. *After all this stress I better at least pass fourth grade.*

The doors to the hall were standing open, just like the front entrance. Sam motioned for us to stop before we reached them, and I hung back as she peered inside. There was a pause, then she stepped right into the doorway.

"There's no one here!" she said, not even trying to keep her voice down.

"Okay," I said. "This is officially creeping me out."

"Same," Sam said, and we wheeled the cart in.

The tryout hall was a big, bright room with high steel-beam ceilings, concrete floors, and a row of picture windows along one wall. On the far side across from the entrance was a stage. And filling the space in between was a total disaster area.

The whole left side was a traffic jam of metal tables on wheels. Lots of the tables had science projects on them, which must have belonged to the kids outside. Some of the projects were glowing or humming, and one of the volcanoes was smoking.

Over on the right side of the room, red-padded chairs were piled up in front of the windows. They'd probably originally been in rows for watching families to sit in, but now they were all knocked over like they'd been through an earthquake.

In the upper-right corner, between the chairs and the stage, there was a heap of technical equipment, and I spotted a camera labeled with the name of the local TV station. It was the gear the news crews had carried on their first trip inside. The crew that had never made it back out.

Just to make everything extra messy, there were red velvet ropes on brass stands tipped over and tangled everywhere. Obviously they'd once been all neat and organized, too, but whatever happened here with the slimebie invasion and escaping kids left them snarled under chairs, wrapped around tables, and sprawled across the floor.

All in all, this was no kind of place for a shopping cart. Especially not a shopping cart balancing a pool of soup that was supposed to save the world. And speaking of . . .

"Hey," I said to Sam. "I thought of something. The slimebies are totally gonna knock this soup over if they all try to eat it at once. Think we should set it on the floor?"

Sam gave me a thumbs-up. "Super-good point," she said. "But I don't think you and I can lift that much soup off the cart and onto the floor without spilling it." She eyed the room. "What about the stage, though?"

I looked. "What *about* the stage?"

"It's like three feet off the floor. We should be able to slide the pool right onto it."

Dang, Sam didn't miss a thing. I gave her two thumbs-up back.

The ropes and chairs and fallen science projects didn't make it easy, but somehow we got the shopping cart through the mess, weaving around obstacles like we were playing the worst-designed video game ever until we had it nosed up against the edge of the stage.

The stage was the fanciest part of the whole room and the only bit that still looked ready for the tryouts. There were banners and backdrops showing Professor Quandary, a fake lab setup with colored liquids in jumbo plastic beakers, and a cloth-covered table on the left where the judges would sit.

"Ready?" Sam asked, bracing one foot behind the cart and hugging her side of the kiddie pool.

"Ready," I said, copying her.

Slowly, carefully, with the weight of the spinach soup burning our arms, we set the kiddie pool down.

"Go, team!" Sam said, raising her hand for a high five. I slapped it but only half-heartedly.

We'd gotten the anti-slimey-dote bait to where it was supposed to be, but where were the slimebies who were supposed to eat it? Shouldn't they have smelled it by now or something?

"Come on," said Sam. "Let's check out the stage while we wait for the slimebies to show up."

We clambered up, and right away Sam marched over to the judges' table and sat behind a sign that said PROFESSOR QUANDARY.

"Well, I think we've seen enough," she said, imitating the professor's sappy TV voice. "There's no doubt about it. You, Samantha Baptiste, are the greatest junior scientist in the country. We're going to have you compete on the national TV show as a formality"—she gave the center of the stage a huge wink—"but I can tell you now, you've already won. Congratulations!"

I fake clapped as she pretended to shake her own hand over the table.

Sam obviously felt right at home up there onstage, but I sure didn't. I felt totally out of place.

I walked to the very center and looked out, picturing the chairs all full of strangers, and the TV cameras running, and the judges asking Sam and me about our project. Sam would give the answers. But what if they wanted me to talk, too? What if they asked me what I'd done to help? Or why I thought I deserved to be up there?

Maybe it was just the mess of the last few days or getting almost zero sleep the night before, but I swore I could feel the hot stage lights burning on my face. I could hear the whispers from the crowd. I could see the judges' frowns and the look in Sam's eyes when I just stood there, opening and closing my mouth like a fish.

Because it turned out I kind of cared.

I cared what they all thought about me. And yeah, maybe I'd actually been doing pretty good these last few days for a change, but did I really deserve to be up there? Was I going to start, like, actually, *seriously* focusing on important things like my parents wanted? Was I going to work hard to become more brave and curious and friendly like Sam? What even mattered most in the end? I didn't know.

So, what could I say?

"Hey, Billy, come and look at this."

It took me a second to blink away the imaginary crowd. I turned around to find Sam crouching down, lifting the cloth covering the judges' table so she could peer under it. I crossed the stage and crouched down beside her. The light from the windows didn't quite reach, but it looked like there were a whole bunch of containers or something hidden under there.

"I hit one with my foot," Sam said. "I wonder . . ." She reached into the semi-darkness and pulled one of the containers into the light.

We both gasped.

It was a bucket, filled almost to the top with glowing, golden slime.

"Oof, okay," I said. "At least we found the slime."

"And it's still gold, so that means it's still un-activated, right?" Sam gave the bucket a small shake so rainbows danced over her face. "I guess that's good news." She frowned. "Only why *haven't* they activated it? Isn't that all it takes to start making more slimebies? What are they waiting for?"

"Maybe they want to find the secret whatever-it-is first?" I said, shrugging. "What I don't get is why they stashed it all under the judges' table." I drummed my fingers on the stage. "I know I should probably mostly be worrying about finding my parents, but something extra weird is going on around here. Even weirder than before, I mean."

Sam sighed. "I can't *stop* thinking about my mom. I bet she was one of the very last grown-ups to get slimebified. That's totally my fault, too. I should have called and warned her from your house. She probably got here early to help us set up. And now . . ."

"Hey, we'll cure her," I said. I didn't like seeing Sam sad. "We'll cure all of them. We made the antidote. We brought it here. We're so close."

"CLOSER THAN YOU THINK!" said a gurgling, screeching voice from just above our heads.

Sam and I whirled around and found Professor Quandary—the real, non-cardboard Professor Quandary—standing over us.

"Oh, hello!" he said, his horrible smile shining. He reached out with both hands, the fingers curled.

"Run!" shouted Sam, and we scrambled to our feet and ran in opposite directions just as Professor Quandary made a swipe for us. We darted around the kiddie pool, narrowly avoiding his grasp, and jumped down from the stage.

And my blood turned to frozen spinach in my veins.

While Sam and I had been distracted by the buckets under the table, the slimebies had arrived.

They were all there—Sam's mom, my parents, Mrs. Hubble, the florist lady, the mayor—too many to count, spread out in a ring around the room, blocking any chance of escape. My heart started trampolining off my ribs when I saw that they'd even closed the doors.

We were shut in and surrounded.

We'd walked straight into a trap.

CHAPTER TWENTY-FOUR

(Sam)

Okay, we were in serious, epic, major trouble, surrounded by a ring of sixty seething, salivating slimebies. But my eyes were glued to just one.

"Mom!"

She was near the windows, backlit by the sunlight. She swayed slightly, but she didn't answer. She looked so pretty. I loved that purple blouse on her, and those were her best fancy-occasion shoes. She'd really dressed up for my big day on the TV tryouts.

And hey, maybe she'd still get a chance to see them. Our plan was working, right? All the pieces were there: The anti-slimey-dote soup was in place; the slimebies were gathered. The tryouts could still happen!

Only why weren't the slimebies rushing the platform to

dive into their favorite meal? Had we made the recipe wrong? Was it not cold enough anymore?

There was a flash of movement in the window behind my mom, and like something out of an animated movie a row of heads rose into view. It was the kids from out front! And Gilbert! And Zack in his purple nose and mustache glasses. They all looked utterly horrified.

But why was nothing happening?

"What's going on?" Billy murmured out of the corner of his mouth. "Why aren't they taking the bait?"

"I was going to ask you the same thing," I hissed back.

We stood shoulder to shoulder, turning a slow circle, taking in the whole silent slimebie army. Finally, we were facing Professor Quandary on the stage again. He stood watching us, looking just as intent and creepy as before, his hands thankfully back at his sides.

"Um, hi, Professor," I called out, trying to sound as confident and brave as I could. "We, uh, made you your favorite soup." I pointed to the kiddie pool full of noxious goo. "Aren't you hungry? Maybe you and your friends here could all take a bite? Tell us what you think?"

Professor Quandary grinned down at us. "Oh, we're hungry," he said. "Hungry to finish our work."

His voice made shivers run down my neck. He had the

same hoarse gurgle as the rest of the slimebies but with enough of his regular smooth TV voice to confuse things. It was like listening to two people talking at once. He almost sounded like he knew what was going on.

"Um, okay," I said. "Wouldn't a snack help you work, though?" Professor Quandary was clearly the head of the slimebies now, and if he ate the soup, hopefully the rest of them would follow.

"We have work to do," said Professor Quandary. He took a step forward.

"*We?*" said Billy loudly. I could tell he was trying to sound brave, too. "Don't you mean *I*? Aren't you even your own person anymore?"

Professor Quandary turned his toothy smile on him. "We are one slime," he said, an extra gurgle in his voice. "But soon there will be more, more, more!"

Professor Quandary turned and yanked the cloth off the judges' table, revealing the buckets of un-activated slime. "Still work to do," he said. "Waiting for the missing ingredient."

He nudged the nearest bucket with his toe and smiled down into it. His voice dropped to a croon, almost singsong.

"And here it is."

Professor Quandary's eyes slid sideways, locking right onto the two of us.

"Billy!" I croaked out as the truth crashed over me like ice water. "I think I know the missing ingredient!"

"What is it?"

"*You!* Remember how the slime only activated when you *touched* it?!"

Billy's face melted into a look of complete horror.

"But then that means the slime wants my—"

"Skin!" shrieked Professor Quandary from the platform. His hands were contorted into claws again, waving madly at the slimebie army. "Bring me their skin!"

And the circle of grinning grown-ups began closing in. Billy and I backed into the center, dodging chairs and velvet ropes to keep our footing.

"Sam! You have to run for it!" Billy yelled. His voice was all high and squeaky. "It's me they want. If I lead them away from the doors, you might be able to—"

"Billy Hamilton, do not try to be a hero!" I yelled back. "Anyway, they're after both of us. Professor Quandary said *their* skin!"

The slimebies were five steps closer now, then six. Gaps appeared as they moved around tables or signs, but they closed too quickly for us to get through. We spun in our tiny circle, looking for any chance.

"Why both of us?" Billy panted. "If the slime knows

everything Professor Quandary knows, then it must know it was me."

"But Professor Quandary didn't know that," I said. "Remember? He got slimebied right as he was asking a question about which of us did something first. I bet you he was asking who touched the slime. He knew it was one of us but not which one!"

The slimebies on the stage had reached the edge. They jumped down, Professor Quandary coming with them. The trap was closing. There was no escape.

"Skins!" screamed Professor Quandary again. "Work to do! Skins!"

"Skins!" the slimebie army echoed back.

Suddenly one of the TV crew slimebies stumbled over a fallen velvet rope. He took the slimebie beside him down as he fell, and she grabbed at the old man slimebie next to her. The three of them crashed to the floor, all fighting to get back up, tangling tighter and tighter.

Billy and I looked at each other. "Run!" we shouted at the same time.

It was our one shot. The anti-slimey-dote had obviously failed. Getting out with our lives and our skins intact was all that mattered now.

Billy was running fast, but I was faster. I jumped over the

knot of tangled slimebies and sprinted for the doors. A second later Billy slammed into them beside me, and we desperately shook the handles.

"No, no!" I yelled. The doors were locked! Billy pounded on them with his fists, but it was no good. We were still trapped.

"Nowhere to run, honeys!" came Professor Quandary's voice from the back of the mob. To my horror I saw my mom step directly on one of the tangled-up slimebies as she marched toward us. Billy made a noise like a sob, and I was willing to bet he'd spotted his parents, too.

"Which way?" I asked. We only had seconds to get away from the doors.

Billy's eyes met mine, and I knew with a sinking feeling that he was realizing the same thing I was: There was no way we could avoid the slimebies forever.

"We'll have to split up, like you said," I decided, making the decision in a flash. "Maybe we can confuse them long enough to find another way out."

"What? No. I don't think—" Billy began, but I cut him off.

"I'll take left, you go right." I gave him a shove toward the windows. "Ready? Now!"

I turned and sprinted along the wall, hoping the sounds I was hearing behind me were Billy doing the same. I risked a glance over my shoulder and felt a surge of excitement. It had worked! The slimebies nearest to the doors had stopped, their heads and hands shifting back and forth, unsure which of us to follow. The ones behind kept pushing, causing the whole mob to pile up in a slimebie traffic jam.

I darted through the maze of tables covered in other kids' projects, finally ducking down out of sight behind a poster about photosynthesis. I scanned the hall from my new position. There *had* to be another exit. A fire escape, or a service entrance, or— Yes! There was a small door to the left of the stage! If Billy and I could get through, then somehow block it behind us . . .

A scream cut through my planning. I jumped up and felt my heart plummet right back down to the floor. The slimebie mob had made up its mind. And it had gone for Billy. He was pressed into the corner by the windows, slimebie hands reaching out to grab everything they could, to tear the skin from his body, maybe even turn him inside out.

Everything was falling apart. And the stage door was right there. I had a clear shot at escape!

But I couldn't go. I couldn't leave Billy.

And even more than that I couldn't let the slimebies win.

I was the only person left who could stop the slimebie takeover of the world.

"SKIN! SKIN!"

The crowd was closing in on Billy. I looked around frantically. How could I save him?

"SAM! HELLLLLP MEEE!"

"Hang on!" I yelled.

It was infuriating. We'd been so close to fixing everything, and now it was all ruined. I kicked the photosynthesis poster in frustration, breaking it in two and knocking over the table next to me, sending a big plastic bottle toppling to the floor. Its cap popped open, and clear liquid glugged out onto the concrete. The familiar stinging smell of vinegar hit my nose.

I jumped back to keep the liquid from reaching my shoes, then— Wait . . . Vinegar!

I spun around again, this time actually taking in all of the abandoned science experiments. The peaks of the baking soda volcanoes suddenly glowed like angels before my eyes. Ideas started forming fast and furious in my brain: physics formulas, chemical combinations, rapid-fire science.

I ran from table to table, gathering what I needed, stacking the volcanoes one on top of the other from biggest to smallest. I felt a little bad I was wrecking all these other kids' projects, but really, this was a save-the-world-level emergency.

"KEEP FIGHTING, BILLY!" I yelled as I crammed the

pieces together. Right in the nick of time I got everything done and smashed my new mega experiment onto its own rolling table. I poured the rest of the bottle of vinegar into the volcano on top, crossed my fingers, and gave the whole thing a hard shove across the room, right past the chairs and tangled velvet ropes, directly into the surging swarm of slimebies.

The impromptu experiment exceeded my wildest expectations.

The top volcano erupted first, sending yellow foam flying and setting off the second volcano with a roar of smoke, sparks, and bubbles. Within five seconds the entire tower of handmade volcanoes was exploding like a technicolor Mt. Vesuvius, and the slimebies were falling down, falling back, totally distracted by the noise and smell and chaos.

I raced across the room, jumping over chairs.

"Billy! Billyyyyyy!"

And there he was, stumbling out of the foam and smoke with slimebies at his heels. I ran for him, ready to lead him to the side door, but instead he grabbed me by the arm. "This way!" he shouted, and he pulled me toward the stage. I had no clue what he was planning, but with foam-flecked slimebies grabbing at us from all sides, there was zero time to ask.

Billy jumped up onto the stage and held out both hands for me just as the slimebies caught us. I ducked a swinging arm; spun around a swaying Mrs. Hubble, her gray hair splattered pink from the volcano blast; locked my fingers with his; and then I was up, beside him on the stage, safe for a few more seconds at least. Maybe we'd be able to see another way out from up here? Maybe that was Billy's plan?

But then I realized Billy was still moving, the momentum of helping me up carrying him backward. There was a jolt and suddenly I was moving, too, Billy's hands still tight around mine as he fell directly into the kiddie pool of icy spinach-slime soup . . . pulling me in with him.

CHAPTER TWENTY-FIVE

(Billy)

Time collapsed into super-slow motion as I fell into the spinach, slow enough for me to see the look on Sam's face as I pulled her in after me. *Oof.* I was going to have some serious explaining to do if we ever got out of this. But I'd figured it out. This was our only hope. The slimebies wanted our skin more than they wanted the soup, so we'd have to put the soup directly in their way.

My whole body tensed as I hit the freezing surface. It was absolutely the worst thing ever. My clothes instantly soaked up the icy water, and the softening clumps of spinach felt like worm guts as they squished under my fingers and elbows and knees.

A heartbeat later Sam was beside me. She flailed, trying to get out, but the anti-slimey-dote made the sides of the kiddie pool slick and she kept falling back, crashing into the liquid slop. In seconds we were both covered from head to toe in green gunk.

"Aaagh!" Sam yelled. "It's in my nose!"

She pulled off her novelty glasses and flung them away, but then her face crumpled as she got a full lungful of what we were sitting in.

She turned to me, eyes blazing, slime and soup dripping down her forehead, and yanked the glasses from my face, too.

"This was your idea, Billy Hamilton!" she yelled over the roaring of the slimebies racing toward us. "We're in this together!"

I wanted to say something brave and heroic, but the putrid smell was foaming into my brain and I couldn't even speak.

This was it: our last chance. We were trapped even worse than before. There was no way we'd be able to run now, all slimy and slippery and oily. We could only sit there, shivering, gagging at the stench, waiting for sixty full-grown, screaming slimebies to reach us.

Something moved in the muck beside me and I almost screamed, too, but it was only Sam, holding out a hand. I took it in mine. We held on tight.

And then the slimebies got us.

CHAPTER TWENTY-SIX

(Sam & Billy)

"AAAAHHHHHHH!!!"
"AAAAHHHHHHH!!!"

CHAPTER TWENTY-SEVEN

(Billy)

Grinning faces surged around us. Slimy hands were every-where. Slimebies crawled over one another to get up onto the stage and into the kiddie pool, where Sam and I twisted and writhed, desperately trying to fight off the grasping fingers and stay above the freezing, gloopy water, both of us yelling and screaming to match the hungry roars of the slimebies.

Those were the very worst moments of my life.

But then, slowly, I realized through all the thrashing and yelling and the brain-melting smell that Sam and I were still in the kiddie pool. And our skin was still attached to our bodies.

The slimebies kept coming, pressing down on us, mouths open and hands flailing, but they couldn't get a grip in the oily mess. And there were new sounds happening: slurping, chewing sounds. Sounds I recognized from that horrible night I found the slimebies feasting in my kitchen.

"No! NO!"

It was the slime's voice, speaking through Professor Quandary.

Through the green haze in my eyes I saw him tugging at the slimebies around us, pulling them away. But they were slippery now, too, and Professor Quandary lost his grip, then his balance, and it was his turn to fall into the pool, face-first and squelching, just missing my kicking feet.

He fought to get out, but more slimebies charged in.

Only there were fewer of them now. Fewer grasping hands and terrifying smiles and crushing bodies.

Fewer and fewer.

Professor Quandary resurfaced, swallowing air and a mouthful of oily spinach as he flopped out over the side.

A handful of slimebies rushed in to fill the gap.

And then only one slimebie was left attacking us.

And then none.

Sam and I stopped flailing, settling to a shaky stop in the last few dregs of soup.

The only sound in the whole entire hall was a soft dripping.

I blinked the spinach slime away from my eyes and saw Sam doing the same.

The slimebies were sprawled out around us. Every one of them was smeared with spinach, slick with oil, and sticky with honey.

None of them were smiling.

Then one of the slimebies near us twitched. A woman, wearing what might have once been nice jeans and an orange top. She twitched, and blinked, and raised a hand to her nose.

She looked over at us in our kiddie pool of evil, and something that might have been recognition flashed in her eyes.

And then she sneezed.

She sneezed like a jet airplane taking off, like a hot air balloon popping, like a rocket launching to the moon . . . and a jet of slime erupted from both her ears, landing on the floor with a squelch.

I gasped and felt Sam's hand clamp onto my arm as another slimebie twitched. Then another. And another.

And then the show began. All through the room slimebies twitched, shuddered, and sneezed, spurts of slime flying out of their ears like the grossest, smelliest, most disgusting fireworks show ever.

In the middle of everything, Professor Quandary hauled himself up beside our pool, making Sam and me jump, and sneezed so hard he almost fell back over. Silver-blue slime squelched out of his ears and splattered to the stage floor, where Sam and I had a good view as it shivered like Jell-O, collapsed, and melted away, leaving a dark brown smear behind it.

Sixty slimebies meant a lot of sneezing, but it couldn't have been more than a minute later when the very last squelching explosion died away. Silence returned to the hall, apart from a few moans from some of the former slimebies.

Sam and I turned to each other right there in the pool, exhaled hard, and high-fived.

We had totally done it! We saved the world!

"What . . . on . . . earth?"

I turned and saw my mom leaning against the judges' table, a hand pressed to the side of her head, smearing the blue-and-silver ooze. Then she spotted me. Her jaw dropped. But before either of us could say a word the doors of the hall flew open with a dramatic bang and a roaring crowd of kids came charging in.

It was every kid we'd seen outside, plus more from the neighborhood. They came charging in like warriors, their fists raised, and at their head was Zack, his fake nose and mustache flashing, his EZ-Shop apron flying, a crowbar in one hand and a cardboard cutout of Professor Quandary lifted like a shield in the other, Gilbert barking at his side.

The rescue party—which I guessed was what it was?—made it a good twenty feet into the hall before they came to a jumbled, tripping halt. A couple of kids sniffed the air, their noses wrinkling, and the next second they were all plugging their noses, yelling, "EWW!" and "GROSS!" and backing away for the exits.

"Who's this guy?" said a member of the TV crew, pointing to Zack. "The Pied Piper of Hamelin?"

"What—what's going on here?" Zack yelled, his eyes darting all around the room, eventually landing on Sam and me right in the center of everything.

"I believe," said a smooth, reassuring voice to my left, "there are some explanations in order." Professor Quandary had gotten to his feet. He ran a hand through his floppy white hair, making it stand up impressively with shiny slimy streaks. He looked like every cartoon version of a friendly mad scientist rolled into one. "And, naturally, I will go first."

CHAPTER TWENTY-EIGHT

(Sam)

"So, are you going to explain exactly why you pulled me into that spinach soup?" I asked.

Billy and I were sitting on an empty rolling table that had once held a volcano, keeping out of the way. We were still soaked, sticky, and extra, extra stinky, but a nice emergency services lady had come around with wet wipes, so at least our faces and hands were clean.

"Sorry, it was all I could think of," said Billy. "The slimebies were screaming about getting our skin, right? So I thought if we put the soup in the way and then let them catch us, they might accidentally eat it. It was worth a shot."

I eyed him. "You mean you observed the slimebies' behavior, made a hypothesis about how to adapt to it, and tested out your idea with an experiment?"

"Yeah . . . Why, is that— Ugh," he groaned. "Did I do science again?"

I gave him a pat on the head.

All around us, the tryout hall was milling with people.

The slimebies had all turned back into super-confused grown-ups who apparently didn't remember a thing. Our parents had rushed over to us as soon as they were back to normal, but now they were with everyone else being interviewed by the emergency services people and the police.

Professor Quandary, after some serious attention from the wet-wipe lady, was being interviewed by the TV crew. Billy and I could hear him talking from our perch on the table.

". . . like I said," he was saying, smiling nonstop, "it was all just a publicity stunt that got the teensy tiniest bit out of hand. A, uh, miscalculation in the chemical composition, you could say." He chuckled enthusiastically, and the TV reporter joined in.

He'd been repeating that story since the first police officers arrived: that everything was fine, and this was all just a surprise twist for the *AMERICA'S GOT SCIENCE* auditions that had gone a little sideways. There was no way the police or TV reporters would have believed the truth anyway, but I was still grateful that he was covering for us.

After all, technically it was all our fault. Everything that had happened started with Billy and me doing unknown science projects from a book labeled TOP SECRET! DANGEROUS! DO NOT TOUCH!

The interview wrapped up and Professor Quandary shook hands with everyone, then excused himself and came right over to us.

"Thanks for not telling them what really happened," I said as he arrived.

He winked. "Not a problem, Sam Baptiste and Billy Hamilton." He tapped his head at the look of surprise on our faces. "Oh, I never forget a name. And it wasn't a total deception I spun over there; this *was* all due to a science experiment gone slightly wrong, wasn't it?"

"*Slightly* wrong?" said Billy.

"Okay, very wrong," Professor Quandary amended. "But I can promise you it is going to make for some world-class publicity! I should be the one thanking you!"

I couldn't help feeling a glow of happiness, even remembering the framed picture in Mariana Hamilton's trunk. Professor Quandary, the world-famous celebrity scientist, was thanking *me*. In person!

"Hey, we know you just did the TV interview," I said. "But we have a few questions, too. If that's okay?"

"Fire away, kids! Fire away!"

I looked at Billy. He was squinting suspiciously at the professor, but he nodded.

"Okay," I said. "First we wanted to know why the slimebies didn't jump on the spinach soup as soon as we got here. Why did you—*they*—stay in hiding? They couldn't keep away from the soup back at Billy's house."

"Ah, well . . ." Professor Quandary folded his arms and leaned against our table. "Am I right in thinking you added the WORLD'S WORST SLIME I told you to make to your spinach soup?"

We nodded.

"An excellent plan," Professor Quandary said. "And I'm sure you noticed that that slime was potent stuff. A little goes a long way, as they say."

I flashed a look at Billy. That was exactly what his grandma had written in her lab book.

"It dampened the smell of the spinach, you see," Professor Quandary continued, "which was certainly a factor. But you may also have noticed that the mind of the WORLD'S MOST POWERFUL SLIME was focused on securing the missing final ingredient. Not on feeding its troops."

"We definitely noticed!" I said. "The slimebies chased us all around the room! I thought we were dead for sure, until Billy had the idea of jumping in the soup."

"A risky plan, but a good one! With you two thrashing around like that in the pool, the slimebies were able to smell the spinach soup again. They still wanted your skin, but from that moment on they wanted the soup more. And the result was quite a frenzy, wasn't it?!" He held his arms wide and smiled, taking in the room. "I'm so glad it worked!"

There was a comfortable silence, but something Professor Quandary had just said was nagging at my mind.

"Hang on," I said. "How do you know Billy and I were thrashing around in the pool? We didn't tell you that."

"Hey, yeah," said Billy. "The only way you'd know that is if you *remembered* being a slimebie! And nobody else does . . ."

Professor Quandary's face went totally blank for a moment, then he calmly shoved the experiment next to us off its rolling table and sat down in its place.

"You kids really are the most remarkable pair of scientists," he said. "And you're right. Unlike the other adults here I *do* remember everything. Please understand, I wasn't in *control*! But I remember."

"How?" I said, just as Billy said, "Why?"

Professor Quandary slowly shook his head. "The only

explanation I can hypothesize is based upon something I've done my best to forget for a long, long time."

"What?" I whispered.

Professor Quandary looked up at us with sad, faraway eyes.

"I've been a slimebie before."

CHAPTER TWENTY-NINE

(Still Sam)

"Our conversation on the sidewalk earlier ended rather abruptly," Professor Quandary said. "So I never got a chance to tell you how I knew your grandmother, Billy."

"We already know," I said. "You and Mariana Hamilton were lab partners."

"We found a picture," Billy added darkly.

I waited to see if Billy was going to share any more details about the picture, but he just stared at the professor, his face blank.

"Oh, that's nice," said Professor Quandary. "And it's true, Mariana and I were lab partners all through college. I owe her a great deal for her support during those years. She was an excellent scientist: brilliant, daring, always taking risks. And I was—well, I had plenty of other things going on in my college life, and I don't know if you two have noticed yet, but sometimes science can just be so much *work*!"

Billy shifted beside me on the table.

"Anyway," Professor Quandary went on, swinging his legs like a kindergartner. "As graduation approached, my grades weren't quite what I needed them to be, and I found myself up against a senior project deadline with nothing to hand in. Mariana and I had just finished an experiment that yielded a beautiful golden, glowing substance we didn't know much about yet, so I, uh, borrowed it. And presented it to my class."

"You didn't," I said.

"I'm afraid I did," said Professor Quandary. "The results were . . . messy. I remember standing in front of the class pouring the beautiful glowing slime out into my hand, then a sort of shivering feeling, then nothing. Not until I came to in the university cafeteria surrounded by rampaging slimebies and Mariana Hamilton standing over me with a spoon. Plus, the most terrible taste in my mouth."

"So, my grandma had to clean up your mess?" said Billy. "She saved the day?"

Professor Quandary nodded. "Entirely. Mariana made the connection between the golden slime missing from our workspace and the chaos the other slimebies and I were causing on campus. She theorized the antidote and put it together. She duct-taped a pair of earmuffs over her ears and led the charge against the army of slimebie college students. She did indeed save the day."

"What happened next?" I asked, whispering without meaning to. "Did you get in trouble?"

"With Mariana, certainly!" Professor Quandary did his chuckle. "She made me sit up all night with her while she filled in her lab book, going over the theory and method for both slimes. She also made me listen to details about what the other slimebies and I got up to. *And* she gave me a lecture on scientific responsibility! It's ironic that she herself gave up science only six months later. For extreme sports, too! It was almost like she was trying to get as far away from science as possible.

"As for the university, they hushed the whole thing up and blamed a combination dishwasher explosion and chemical leak in the cafeteria."

"You didn't get in trouble with the school at all?" asked Billy. He had a deep line between his eyebrows.

Professor Quandary looked super guilty for a second, then hitched his smile back on. "Ah, well. Yes. The next day I did receive word that I would not be graduating until I'd repaid the school for damages."

"How long did that take?" I asked.

Professor Quandary waved a hand vaguely. "Oh, you know," he said. "Things worked out." He looked out across the hall, humming loudly to himself.

I looked out, too. Beside the stage was a stack of empty buckets, all that was left after the Conference Center janitors poured the un-activated WORLD'S MOST POWERFUL SLIME carefully down a mop sink. I blinked.

"Hey, something else I still don't get," I said. "If the slimebies had that whole bathtub full of new slime ready, why didn't they activate it?"

Professor Quandary stopped humming. "Strange but true scientific fact," he said, "slimebies can't activate slime. It's simply not possible."

"Whoa," I said. "But then why not get someone else to activate it? There were plenty of non-slimebies here for the contest. Why did you—*they*—only want to use Billy?"

Professor Quandary beamed. He seemed really happy for the change of subject.

"Well, now we're getting into what you might call the *psychology* of the slime," he said. "The original slime you two made and activated had, essentially, one mind. One mind it could spread among sixty or so bodies. To make more of *itself*, it needed new slime activated with the same key ingredient as the first one."

"My skin," said Billy.

"Your skin." Professor Quandary nodded. "If they'd let someone else activate it, the new slime would have become a totally *different* slime, with a different mind. It would have been a competitor, trying to make slimebies of its own."

A whole other batch of living slime with a whole other agenda? I didn't even want to think about what kind of mess that would have caused. We'd barely managed to escape from the mess we already had.

"So what would have happened if the slimebies had actually won?" I asked, shuddering a little at the memory of all those screams and smiles and clawing hands. "Would Billy and I have, you know, died?"

"Heavens no, not *both* of you!" Professor Quandary waved a hand. "No, Billy would have been kept around for as long as possible. Years, even. I imagine the slimebies would have kept him in some sort of vat, constantly dumping new slime in for him to activate." He beamed at Billy. "You might have gotten to see the world as they rampaged for slime components and final global conquest! If they put a window in your vat, that is!"

"Great," said Billy faintly. He squinted at Professor Quandary, then took a deep breath and raised his hand.

"Billy?" Professor Quandary said, calling on him like a teacher in class.

"I was just wondering," Billy said. He was speaking very carefully. "If you had so much trouble in college, since, you know, science was a whole lot of work and all . . . how did you come up with the design for the Hyper-Quantum Telescope right after? It's just, it must have been super complicated, and there's this one section missing from my grandma's lab book, and I think—"

Professor Quandary's famous face went five shades paler in under a second, and he jumped up from his rolling cart so fast you'd think he'd been electrocuted.

"Attention, everyone! Attention, please!" he shouted, cutting Billy off, his voice echoing across the room. "May I have everyone's attention? Switch those television cameras back on, my friends. You'll want to get this!"

Billy's extra-wide eyes met mine. What was happening? Obviously Billy had hit the nail on the head, and the origins of the Hyper-Quantum Telescope were something Professor Quandary did *not* want to talk about. But had Billy gone too far? Was Professor Quandary about to turn the tables on us? Spill the beans? Tell the emergency workers and police and our parents and everyone that we were the ones to blame for all of this? Were we not gonna be allowed to graduate fourth grade until we'd paid off all the damages, too?

When the hall was quiet and every eye was on him, Professor Quandary spoke, using his very smoothest TV voice.

"Friends, fans, families, I have a truly *wonderful* announcement to make. As you know, the little something extra we had planned for this stop on the *AMERICA'S GOT SCIENCE* National Junior Tryouts Tour has gone a tiny bit, uh, outside the lines." He led the audience in a chuckle. "But by a remarkable and lucky coincidence, the very problem we experienced was solved thanks to a feat of ingenious and quick-thinking science, performed by none other than your own, your very own, Sam Baptiste and Billy Hamilton!"

He swept out an arm, presenting us to the crowd, and there was a wave of applause and cheering. Billy and I sat there, frozen, totally confused.

"And I am even more happy to announce," cried Professor Quandary, holding up both hands, "that in honor of their outstanding achievement, I am hereby declaring these exceptional young scientists the winners of this regional competition! And they will be joining me live on national television for the *AMERICA'S GOT SCIENCE* Junior Grand Championships in three months' time!"

This time the crowd exploded, everyone rushing forward

to congratulate us, shaking our hands and patting us on the back. Billy's mom and dad jumped in to squeeze him from both sides in a massive hug, and my mom appeared, picking me up and spinning me in circles, yelling, "That's my girl!"

Eventually the TV crew managed to drag us over to the camera alongside Professor Quandary.

"Here's our heroic duo!" Professor Quandary said loudly as the TV crew fussed over some problem with the lighting. "I hope they're ready to work hard preparing for the competition!" He suddenly leaned down so our heads were together, dropping his voice to a whisper. "But just between us friends, so long as we, uh, *have each other's backs* and *leave the past in the past*, I can say with real confidence that I already know who's going to take home the grand prize."

Then he straightened back up, smiled at us, and winked.

CHAPTER THIRTY

(Billy)

I felt like I'd fallen smack into the kiddie pool of freezing spinach soup again.

Had Professor Quandary just guaranteed we were going to be the winners of *AMERICA'S GOT SCIENCE*? I looked over at Sam. Sam looked over at me.

Before either of us could react, the news crew started their interview. It only lasted a few minutes, but it felt like way longer, even though Professor Quandary did all the talking while Sam and I just stared at the camera in shock. The producer guy kept motioning for us to smile, and by the end he was getting pretty annoyed that we wouldn't.

The TV crew moved outside after the interview, and Sam and I tried to escape, but there were still so many people congratulating us and asking questions that we barely moved from our corner of the hall. Our parents came rushing back in, of course. Sam's mom squeezed my hand and told me I was definitely getting enough extra credit to pass fourth grade after this, and my mom and dad wouldn't stop hugging me and telling me they were so proud of all my hard work and accomplishments.

It was weird. I knew they didn't really even know what had happened, but I'd never seen them smile so much, and definitely not because of *me*.

I guess I hadn't known how much I needed that.

Professor Quandary disappeared for a while during all the fuss. When he came back he was clean and wearing a whole new change of clothes.

"One of the advantages of having my luggage here with me," he said, pointing at his bags. "And speaking of luggage, my cab will be here any minute, kids. Would you do me the honor of walking me out?"

"I guess," said Sam.

"Do you want help carrying those?" I asked, because my parents were right there.

Professor Quandary jumped like I'd poked him with a pin. "No! No, thank you." He scooped up his three bags in both arms. The last one seemed extra heavy. "I can manage."

We left our parents chatting in the hall and walked back through the long halls of the Conference Center, finally emerging into the normal, everyday, sunny Saturday afternoon. The TV crew was interviewing Zack and some of the kids outside the entrance. Zack was still wearing his novelty nose and mustache.

"Hey, Zack Grocer!" I called as we passed. Zack looked over, and I tapped my nose.

Zack stared at me, then gasped and whipped off his glasses. "Was I seriously wearing these on live TV?" we heard him wail to the interviewer. "Why didn't you tell me?"

We passed a knot of kids next, and I spotted the two girls from our class nudging each other.

"Hey! Sam!" one of them said, taking half a step toward us. "Nice, uh, nice going!"

"With, you know, the contest! And TV! And everything!" said the other.

A small smile appeared on Sam's face.

"See you on Monday, maybe?" called the first girl. "At lunch?"

Sam gave the two girls a shrug and a lazy sort of wave. The smile on her face grew even bigger as we walked away.

I looked around at the sound of barking and spotted

Mrs. Hubble and Gilbert off to our left. The dog was leaping up and down, barking happily in between licking spinach and slime off his owner.

"Get off, you silly beast," I heard Mrs. Hubble grumble. But she scratched his ears fondly with her wrinkly fingers, forgetting to keep up her usual scowl.

Professor Quandary's cab was already waiting for us when we reached the curb. The driver got out to help with the bags, and I blinked, trying to remember: Did Professor Quandary have this much luggage when he arrived?

"Well, goodbye for now, my young scientists!" he said, wiping his forehead. "So much has happened since this morning when I found you two waiting for me! I'm glad we met! And I'm *so* glad we *understand* one another." He winked again. "Until next time!"

He slid into the cab and we watched as it pulled away, Professor Quandary's white hair shining from the back seat until Sam and I were staring down an empty road.

"Okay," I said to Sam. "So I know Professor Quandary is a lying, dishonest cheater and this totally isn't what I should be focusing on right now, but I cannot believe we're actually going to win the show! We're going to win the grand prize! One million dollars! Each!"

Sam laughed so hard she started coughing. "Billy, did you

ever read the contest rules?" she said as she recovered. "The grand prize of *AMERICA'S GOT SCIENCE* is a set of books and beakers. You know, research stuff."

All my excitement drained away like golden slime down a mop sink.

"What?" I said. "No million dollars? We're just going to win a bunch of scientific equipment?"

"*I'm* going to win a bunch of scientific equipment," Sam corrected me. "You already have your grandma's." She squinted back down the road. "And we shouldn't be winning it anyway. This whole thing is one big lie. I mean, what's the point of going if the contest is rigged? We didn't even win fair and square today! We both know Professor Quandary was just trying to keep us quiet."

"And I guess it kind of worked," I said, feeling pretty mixed up about that.

"For now, maybe," said Sam. "But we'll see."

Suddenly a voice cut in behind us. "Hey! Hey! Have you two seen Professor Quandary?"

We looked around. Artificial-seaweed girl was running over to us. Her eyes were red, and it looked like she was trying really hard not to cry.

"He left just a minute ago," I said. "We watched him drive away."

The girl's face crumpled. Tears started running down her cheeks.

"Oh, what's wrong?" asked Sam. "Did you want an autograph or something?"

"No!" said the kid. "It's my science project! My dad took me home so he could change out of his slimy clothes, and when we came back to get my project, it was gone!"

I looked at Sam. "You didn't add this kid's seaweed project to your volcano bonfire, did you?"

Sam glared at me. "I wouldn't destroy an experiment that cool! I knew what I was doing!" She patted the girl on the shoulder. "I'm sure it's somewhere inside," she said. "You know, a lot of stuff got piled together and—"

"No!" said the girl. "You don't understand!" She sniffed and swallowed hard. "I checked on it before we left, and it was fine. And I figured nobody would touch it 'cause it was really heavy. Only when we came back, the table was *empty*, and this was there instead."

She held up a shiny piece of paper the size of a postcard.

Dear contestant:

Thank you for entering the AMERICA'S GOT SCIENCE regional competition. While we

```
regret to inform you that your entry
was not chosen, we hope this experience
will set you on the path of science for
many years to come.

Per the rules listed on the entry form,
your project and accompanying research
are now the intellectual property of the
Quandary Enterprise Corporation.

Thank you again for your participation.
```

Sam looked like she wanted to set the card on fire. "Are they *serious*?" she yelled. "I figured that part of the rules was just, like, a formality!"

"What part?" I said.

"There was this section in the fine print that said something like *All entries shall become the property of the Quandary Enterprise Corporation*, blah, blah, blah. I noticed it when I read the form, but I never, ever thought Professor Quandary would *use* it. I mean, it's basically, like, legal theft! Did he take a bunch of other people's stuff, too?" she asked the girl.

"Only . . . mine . . ." the girl said, her words barely getting out through her crying. "Now . . . nobody will know . . .

that I made up . . . artificial seaweed . . . and . . . adapted the . . . cyclonic polymer . . . matrix . . . so it would run . . . on moonlight, too . . . and not just . . . the su-u-un!"

The girl broke down completely, crying so hard that tears were squirting straight out of her eyes.

"Shh," said Sam. "It'll be okay, we'll find a way to fix it." She took the girl by the hand. "Come on, let's go find your dad."

When Sam got back she looked angrier than I'd ever seen her.

"That kid's project was total genius," she said. "It was the best one here. I'll bet anything that's why Professor Quandary took it."

"Hey, that must have been what was in his extra bag!" I said. "Remember he only had two this morning? He carried it out right past us." I shook my head. "First that cheater starts his career by stealing the Hyper-Quantum Telescope from my grandma. Now he's stealing experiments from kids who enter his contest. I bet he's taking projects from kids all over the country, all so he can sell them as his!"

Sam and I crossed our arms in unison.

"What do you think?" I said. "Should we try to expose him?"

"Oh, *absolutely*," said Sam. "But let's do it on live TV

right in the middle of his big dishonest, fake, idea-stealing show! We just need to come up with a project as a cover."

"My grandma's lab book must have something that'll help us win the contest *and* prove what a fraud Professor Quandary is," I said. "It'll probably be hard, but like my, um"—I felt myself going pink—"you know, like my best friend once said, let's see what we can do."

Sam's face lit up brighter than the sun blazing overhead. "Best friend lab partners!" she said, giving me the greatest high five in the entire history of the world. "Too bad Professor Quandary tried to bribe *us*. You and I are the greatest junior scientists ever!"

I smiled back at Sam. "And the whole world is gonna know it."

Acknowledgments

Enormous, slimy, glowing thanks to Jeffrey West, David Levithan, Alex Kahler, Baily Crawford, Caroline Flanagan, the whole team at Scholastic Book Fairs, and my third-grade teacher, Ms. Karwan, who read to us every day and completely changed my life.

About the Author

Liam Gray has never made a batch of zombifying slime, but he did try to invent green peppermint yogurt pops when he was nine and created something that smelled so bad he had to spray all the pans out with the garden hose. He also got sent to the principal's office in fifth grade for having too many nonschool books in his desk, which just might have influenced his decision to become an author and add even more books to the world.

YOUR FAVORITE BOOKS COME TO LIFE IN A BRAND-NEW DIGITAL WORLD!

- Meet your favorite characters
- Play games
- Create your own avatar
- Chat and connect with other fans
- Make your own comics
- Discover new worlds and stories
- And more!

Start your adventure today! Download the **HOME BASE** app and scan this image to unlock exclusive rewards!

SCHOLASTIC.COM/HOMEBASE

MSCHOLASTIC